Torn Symmetry

Torn Symmetry

ROHINI S. BHAMBI

LIBRARY TALES PUBLISHING

Library Tales Publishing

www.LibraryTalesPublishing.com

Copyright © 2025 by Rohini S. Bhambi, All Rights Reserved

Published in New York, New York.

For technical support, please visit www.LibraryTalesPublishing.com

Library Tales Publishing also publishes its books in a variety of electronic formats. Every content that appears in print is available in electronic books.

* * *

9 7 9 8 8 8 9 4 4 1 0 3 5 7

Printed in the United States of America

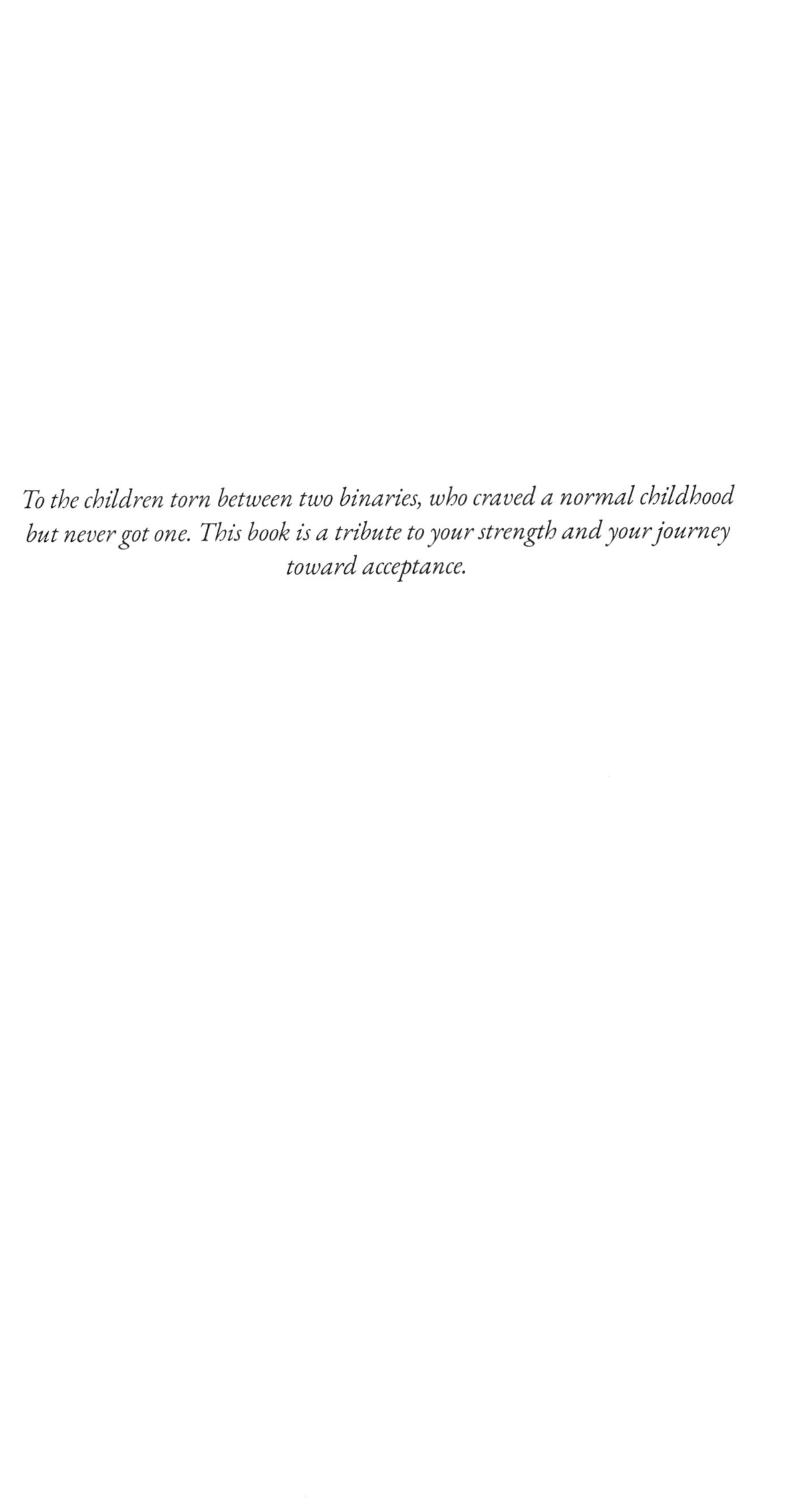

To the children torn between two binaries, who craved a normal childhood but never got one. This book is a tribute to your strength and your journey toward acceptance.

One

✢

THE UNDESIRABLE BOY

Verdi Mansion, Nelson
Feb 21, 1992

It's time. The stygian sky is starless, proudly holding the portentous puffs that have transformed into nimbostratus, ready to unleash a vehement storm. A malefaction is being planned in Verdi Mansion, and nature provides the perfect secrecy to execute the deed. The snow begins to kiss the ground as quietly as possible, diminishing clarity like a dream-like haze. While Nelson bathes in swirls of pure white, Samantha Verdi believes she is still dreaming, though she awoke from the realm of Swevens a while ago—a sleep as short as forty winks, never sufficient to lull her into complete rest.

She can never rest. From the day she birthed her husband's scion, she has lived in constant fear, for the child she has produced is "undesirable."

Samantha sits in her bed, startled and frenzied, her heart racing against the ivory arches. Her jaded eyes scour the room of a prodigious mansion where everything is regal—architecture and furniture alike boast ever-so-inimitable treasures—an abode that is about to be snatched from the youngling resting peacefully in a cot next to her bed.

If one seeks an example of the phrase "sleep like a baby," look no

1

further than young Nathan, a cherub in disguise, swaddled in his cot, sleeping for what seems like an eternity. Ever since birth, he has possessed an equanimous bearing, seldom wailing even when famished.

She wonders sometimes: What has she done to deserve him? With a face glowing like the moon, eyes as round as orbs, lips as pink as peonies, and ears... protruding, just like his father's.

But Robert does not care about physical traits; he cares about genetics. And here, the scandalous genes have mutated, leaving Nathan—a male crafted by chromosomal decree—torn between two binaries.

To Samantha, her son is perfect. Yet beneath the pretense of perfection that eludes the maternal ideals she holds dear, a profound dread lurks, bound by fate and societal norms. This dread, the night hag, has stolen the sweet sleep from her eyes, drowning her in a whirlpool of disquiet and wrestling from her the very essence of the mother she yearns to be for young Nathan: the fear of losing her child.

The door creaks open. The noise of the groaning hinges rises in pitch, just like Samantha's racing heartbeat.

She turns her attention toward the door, where she sees a man lunging in her direction, hastened strides, a cigar alight in his left hand. The room now smells of tobacco. Samantha shields her nostrils from the noxious fumes.

"Are you serious, Robert?" She coughs as the smoke swirls in her lungs. "Smoking inside? It's not good for the baby. How many times do I have to tell you that?"

Hurling her arms over Nathan's cot, she tries to devise a way to protect his tiny nostrils from inhaling the toxic vapors.

The man, clad in his modish garments, continues to weave rings of smoke from his cigar, heedless of her objections, unmoved by how it may hurt others in the room. He adjusts his fedora, advances a few paces toward Samantha, and looks her in the eye.

"Don't worry. He won't stay here for long. Do you know why?"

Samantha swallows, trying to gulp the lump that has welled up in her throat. *Please don't.*

Robert cracks a devious smile, his fingertip gripping the fedora's edge. "Because it's time. The baby needs to go," he says without a trace of sentiment, his dark eyes bleak and dour.

"No!" Samantha squeals, careful not to startle baby Nathan. She perches softly on the edge of the bed. "I beg you," she entreats, her palms pressed together in a quiet plea to the father who stands a world away from the role of Nathan's father.

"I gave you eight months, didn't I?" he says, draping himself onto the bed. The bed squeaks as Robert settles into it.

Samantha blanches, wrapping her arms around herself, her eyes glistening with fear and agony—not for herself, but for the child who was born from her essence.

"He's just a baby, your son, Robert," Samantha says earnestly. "Your child."

Robert grins viciously, the shadowed arc of his smile accentuating the elongated structure of his face. However, his eyes remain downcast, tracing the woven carpet patterns on the floor, the cigar angled between the embers' guardians.

"The baby needs to go," he repeats. "I'll leave now." His voice is gravelly and urgent. "Get him ready."

Samantha springs from the bed, drawn to the cot like a moth to light, lifting the baby and wrapping him against her chest. Time presses in, yet she refuses to release this fragile bundle.

If she could, she'd carve a hollow in her chest to cradle him within forever; if she could, she'd carry him back in the bloom of her own womb; and if she could, she'd flee to distant havens, far from Robert, far from the suffocating world.

But she's trapped, bound by invisible chains to a life she chose herself, her strength faltering as she knows she is incapable of raising her son alone. She is indecisive and unskilled, one who relinquished her freedom when she became Samantha Verdi, unaware it would cost her own identity.

She recalls the moment at the altar when the fervor of becoming a Verdi shimmered in her eyes; how excited she was to renounce her last name at the prospect of affluence and prestige, only for it now to flicker like a fading fire.

Bound by the stringent laws of the family she married into, she yearns for an alternate reality where marriage never penned its binding contract upon her life. She glances at her husband, who had vowed to protect her from all miseries, now the architect of her anguish.

A world was promised to her, woven with joy's golden threads, and she had envisioned herself tending to cozy kin, a home rife with laughter and the pitter-patter of little feet. But here she stands, holding her first-born after a five-year quest nearing surrender, now on the verge of giving him up because her husband won't accept "faulty" children. It's a disgrace to the family.

But she thinks otherwise: it's a disgrace to humanity.

"Samantha, hurry up." Robert leaps from the bed angrily. "I must get rid of him tonight."

"Please, Robert," Samantha begs, inaudible to Robert's unfeeling ears. "Let him grow up in this home. It's his home."

Robert remains an unyielding monolith, impervious to any sway, standing firmly, his decision as solid as the marble floors beneath his feet.

"Please, don't take him," Samantha cries, her voice brittle, drifting like a withered leaf in the precursor winds, her arms outstretched in desperation to shield Nathan from his father.

A drawn-out sigh escapes Robert's mouth as he pitches his cigar onto the floor, besmirching the moonlit quartz. His feet move slowly toward Samantha and Nathan, heels clunking with every step, a harrowing cadence amplifying the dread and despair in Samantha's heart.

Robert's hands reach for Nathan, who remains quietly swaddled in his blanket, and with a forceful yank, he snatches him from her arms, ignorant of his fragility. Samantha gasps, fearing Robert has snapped his neck due to the brutal way he snatched him. Yet, in miraculous resilience, no cries escape the baby.

Samantha continues to plead, clinging desperately to Robert's feet, her fingers slipping, tears streaming down her face. "Please, he is our son," she laments. Her voice becomes shrill, yet her pleas dissipate into thin air.

"Get off me, Samantha," Robert says, attempting to free himself from her. But she clings to him tenaciously, like a lizard to a wall.

"I'll let go of the baby. I'm warning you."

And that was enough: a ringing threat sufficient to persuade Samantha to release her grip. She loosens her hold, allowing Robert to carry out the cruel separation he has planned for eight months.

She remains on the ground, a gaping maw silently conveying her disbelief. The words are menacing, disheartening, and far from fatherly.

Robert places the child on the bed and kneels beside Samantha, now reaching for her face. Without hesitation, his brawny hands tightly grab her cinched bun, pulling her face toward him. With eyes ablaze with wrath, he says, "Get ready. You'll come along to drop this filth."

The grip tightens, constricting Samantha's vessels. She looks at baby Nathan, now peacefully asleep, bowing to his fate. Her chest is heavy, burdened with nature's nectar and melancholia.

She knows Nathan is hungry, yet she cannot bring herself to feed him. A powerless woman, her protest stifled, her insides shriek in a savage frenzy, mourning the death of the mother within her. She gulps her anguish, her eyes begging for mercy, but Robert does not let go of her and proceeds to scoop her up off the floor.

Being so frail, she almost soars toward the ceiling, but Robert's hold is staunch—capable of ripping hair follicles apart—and he succeeds in doing so. As he releases his grip, he unweaves a fistful of hair from her scalp, which falls to the ground, bedewed with blood.

Samantha weeps, horrified at the sight before her. The blood drips down her neck as she collapses on the floor, wan and defeated.

"Get up!" Robert bellows. "We don't have much time."

A trail of tears marks Samantha's cheeks as she lies helplessly on the floor in dual agony, both in flesh and spirit.

Robert leans over again. "Had you given me a proper son, this wouldn't have happened."

Samantha whimpers, her eyes red like a bloodshot sunset, her nose tinged scarlet like fiery autumn leaves.

"You're lucky I'm keeping you here," Robert continues. "For what your womb has done is unforgivable."

He snorts and shakes his head but then falls silent, though his breaths grow louder, like a bull preparing to attack. Samantha watches him from the corner of her eye, sensing his footsteps draw closer, and then he does something grotesque, as if a monster has been unleashed within him: he drives his foot deep into Samantha's stomach.

It rends her spirit, and she growls in pain and humiliation. The intensity of the pain leaves her uncertain of its source, whether it stems from her still-healing womb or the ache deep within her heart. The latter is undoubtedly stronger.

Robert plops down in a chair. Numb from the pain, Samantha rises slowly, massaging her wounded belly as she reaches for her shawl underneath the pillows. Wrapping it around herself, she ignores both the blood trickling from her head and Robert, who sits in the lounge chair with his ankles crossed, devoid of any remorse

With neither reluctance nor fear, she picks up Nathan and brings him to her bare chest. As if instinctively, Nathan's lips part and latch onto her nipple, drawing her milk and savoring her love. Perhaps this moment encapsulates everything.

Nathan falls asleep again. *At least he is fed*, Samantha thinks.

She straightens her dress while still holding Nathan and walks toward Robert. "Ready," she says.

"Good." He rises sharply from the chair. "Make sure your head is covered," he instructs, raising a forefinger. "Don't want a scene here."

Samantha veils her head with the shawl, hiding her wounded scalp from view. This is important to Robert, but her well-being is not. Yet she doesn't care about her contusion; it merely hints at Robert's barbarism and is far from the worst she endures.

She follows Robert out of the room and into the foyer. The staff is absent; Robert has sacked them all. After Nathan's birth, he ensured that no one remained on-site permanently. He hired daytime cooks and cleaners but no nanny. Samantha doesn't need a nanny anyway; she is more than enough for her child.

"After we get rid of him," Robert says, quickening his pace, "I'll hire permanent staff. You won't have to worry about anything. Okay?"

Samantha remains silent.

He turns his head. "Okay?"

His "okay" feels more like a demand for agreement, but Samantha keeps her eyes on Nathan. Though she hears him, she merely nods. What else can she say?

She is least interested in his plans to procure staff for her. What will she do with them when she no longer has her baby? She casts a disdainful glance at his back, but he does not see her.

A shimmering green vase on an oak cabinet in the hallway catches her eye, stirring memories from the depths of her mind: a gift from her husband, bought during their honeymoon in Rome—a fleeting moment when good things filled her life.

That same vase ignites a fierce urge to strike Robert with it, knocking him senseless for good. She reaches for the vase as she nears the cabinet, her hands moving instinctively. But Robert turns around, and her hands retreat.

Some sense begins to penetrate her mind as she considers the repercussions had she indeed hit him. Still, she smiles imagining him sprawled on the floor, prostrate in blood, the police arresting her and tarnishing her existence with the taint of a murderer. But she thinks she could live with that.

Then it strikes her: What will happen to Nathan? He will be taken away from her. She reconsiders the options. If she flees immediately, and the authorities fail to find her, she could live the life of her dreams. But her heart takes a dip again, and questions start to swarm: How will she care for the baby? She lacks the funds, skills, and everything in between.

Robert opens the door and steps outside, not bothering to wait or hold it ajar for her. He rarely does. Samantha wonders if Robert is truly her man. Correction: Is he really a man?

Samantha had dreamed of marrying the most endearing man on earth. For a time, she believed she had found him. Robert is likely the dream man of any woman—tall, handsome, and well-to-do—a renowned builder in British Columbia. Every vein in her body was filled with adoration for him.

The man she thought she married was once drenched in affection, but his true nature emerged over time, revealing a side she had never seen before. At times, he resembles a vulture, preying on human emotions, much like the unsettling display he just exhibited.

Still, her rational mind occasionally contradicts her, questioning whether her feelings are rooted in his inherent goodness or directly proportional to his wealth. In some secluded corner of her heart, Samantha knows the answer.

"Sit in the car," Robert commands, locking the door.

Thick flurries accumulate heavily on the ground. Nelson has become a winter wonderland, painted in pristine white. The prancing of flakes brings cold as an auxiliary unease. Yet for Samantha, it is a comfort, especially for her freshly wounded scalp. She removes her shawl, allowing the cold air to remedy her physical damage, though it cannot heal the wounds of her soul. Lightly clad and without a coat, she welcomes the frigid gusts that brush against her bare arms.

However, she does not feel the cold; an inferno rages inside her, capable of defying the frosty exterior. This inner fire is fueled by her dying motherhood, emitting warmth for the impending journey.

She waits for Robert to open the door, and he does so—not out of care, but exasperation.

"I told you to sit inside."

"I'm holding the baby," she responds, her tone firm.

"Ah, of course, your highness! I forgot you're holding the baby," Robert retorts, slamming the door shut after she finally sits inside. "Holding the fucking baby."

Samantha fights the urge to respond. *Don't say anything, just don't,* she thinks. But her heart fails to comply, and the silver rivers begin to flow, her mouth unable to close as she makes uncontrollable sounds.

"Oh, stop bawling like that," Robert yells, his hands gripping the steering wheel as he waits for the engine to warm up. "Just shut your mouth. Don't make my life worse." He takes deep breaths, clenches his teeth, and then says, "I wish I had just gotten a daughter—a proper daughter."

Samantha gathers herself, trying her best to resist the urge to weep. Gazing outside through the frost-kissed glass, she watches the snow's silent fall.

"You're heartless, Robert," she whispers.

Robert ignores her comment.

The temperature drops further. The car windows fog up. Nathan rests in Samantha's lap, his eyes closed, snug and warm, oblivious to the ominous events ahead. Suddenly, he shudders, his little feet protruding from the blanket. Samantha tucks them back in. She has forgotten the shoes, but he is a stranger in this world of footfalls. What does he need shoes for?

Anxiety swirls in her mind, and with a deep breath, she turns to Robert. "Shouldn't we get the car seat?"

Robert turns his head, and Samantha quickly seals her lips.

"He is safe in your lap."

"No," she insists. "I mean, where do we put him? We need a basket or a car—"

"Oh!" Robert scoffs. "Got a bit of a brain, do you? I thought you were empty." He taps on his temples. "Here."

Samantha remains quiet.

"It's in the trunk. Don't stress yourself over it too much. I have it figured out."

The engine has warmed up. Robert focuses intently on the gauge. The time has come to rid himself of the child he loathes, to resume his normal life, and to purge his estate of the doom Nathan has brought.

He presses down on the accelerator and drives away. The city is sheathed in white; the roads are unclear and slippery, and the lampposts are lit with a meager light. The path is desolate, devoid of vehicles, even snowplows. Yet amidst the eerie silence, a gritty chorus arises—the sound of salt melting the snow and the resulting slush composing a rugged melody beneath the tires.

Robert veers left at the upcoming signal, nearing their destination. The car nearly skids on the black ice, but he deftly handles the vehicle, stopping near an old Victorian building, its details obscured by the darkness.

A few stairs lead up to this building. Robert exits the car and opens the trunk. A biting gust rushes into the warm vehicle. From its depths, he retrieves a car seat, then closes the trunk. Samantha watches him hop toward the building like a frog leaping from lily pad to lily pad. He sets the car seat near the entrance and races down the steps.

Samantha knows it's time.

Robert returns and opens the door. "Come out," he says.

Samantha hesitates, holding Nathan close to her, inhaling the scent of her baby, untouched by time. His fragrance is pure, like the first light of dawn. She is aware of the clock ticking and Robert's growing impatience. She must exit the vehicle but feels compelled to bid her baby a final farewell, lavishing him with kisses.

Robert rolls his eyes and commands, "Come out now!"

A dire urgency compels Samantha to comply. She steps out of the car, her feet sinking into the wintry powder, a shiver shooting up her spine. She trudges with baby Nathan in her arms to the doorstep of the building, where the car seat awaits.

Nathan stirs from slumber but remains in a tranquil state. His round, beady eyes watch the snowflakes dance against a violet backdrop, some landing on his cheeks. He smiles. Seeing him awake makes Samantha more anxious about leaving him alone.

"Robert, he is awake!" she alerts him.

Robert grimaces. "So what?" Then he abruptly reaches for Nathan, disregarding her concern. "Give him to me."

He places Nathan in the chariot of the young voyagers—an infant car seat—preparing him to face the world on his own. But for now, he must adopt the tether, or he could roll over and commence his journey sooner than expected.

Robert straps him in. Nathan doesn't mind, nor does he cry. He is happy to be outside, his joyful glimmer vivifying his surroundings. Yet Robert does not want to see that joy, the radiant smile, or the love Nathan holds for his father.

Quickly, Robert throws a blanket over him, save for his face, averting his eyes from the blossom of his brood, the very pulse of his lineage. He retrieves a letter from his coat pocket and tucks it under Nathan's blanket.

"Go sit in the car," he tells Samantha. "I'll knock on the door, and we'll leave. All right?"

Samantha adjusts her shawl and leans over the seat again but cannot summon the strength to look into her son's eyes. She merely kisses his head—tucked into a hat that she knitted herself—then sprints toward the car.

With three loud knocks, Robert alerts the inhabitants of the building before hurrying back to his car. Without further ado, he speeds off, leaving Nathan alone at the doorstep of Whispering Hearts.

Samantha's heart shatters in desolation. She is on her way back home, but without her baby.

Robert glances at her through the rearview mirror. "I'm sorry, Sam. Sorry to put you through this."

Samantha weeps uncontrollably, thrusting her head against the seat repeatedly, punishing herself so that the wound hurts more—more than her heart hurts at the moment.

"It had to be done," Robert says, a tinge of remorse present in his voice.

Samantha wonders about the freshly revealed side of Robert, emerging amidst the tails of his darker self. It's as if a hidden chapter of his personality is unfolding, contrasting sharply with his usual depravity.

She sees through his façade, aware that he has achieved his goal of separating her from her child, while deriding the womb that carried his child.

"What makes you think you can fix what you've done?" Samantha shouts, her chapped lips cracking further.

Robert remains unfazed and quiet, displaying no signs of disturbance. The "faulty" child now lies at fate's uncertain mercy. She prays for a kind soul to rescue him from the doorstep and accept and cherish him as he deserves.

"Will someone open the door?" she asks, her stomach plummeting at the thought of her baby lying alone in the cold, in the snow.

"I hope so," Robert replies nonchalantly.

"What do you mean you *hope so*? He is our son! We left him in the cold."

"He is no son of mine," Robert barks. "I told you to leave him in the summer, a few weeks after he was born. Didn't I?"

"A newborn, Robert? How can you be so cruel?"

Robert emits a huff of breath. "Don't blame me. You are the one who chose to delay. I told you many times and begged you to let me handle the situation, but you refused."

Samantha sighs and expects such cruelty from him.

"It's your fault now," Robert says.

"But—"

"We are moving to Kamloops by the end of this month, so you can't come back here and check on him."

"How can I not?" Samantha whimpers, collapsing into her seat as if her soul has left her body.

Robert turns right, pulling into the driveway of Verdi Mansion. "Because he's not worth worrying about. It's up to his fate—whoever takes him first, whether it be the orphanage or the winter."

Two

⚬

HOUSE OF THE UNLOVED

Whispering Hearts Orphanage, Nelson
August 12, 1999

In a place where hopelessness persists in the milieu and woe's pall falls long and deep, there exists a bastion of forsaken souls—an orphanage, a citadel of the heart's desolation, a dominion of melancholy—preserving within its walls the somberest of tears, the longest of waits, the deepest of sorrows, the loneliest of sighs, and the heaviest of heartbreaks.

Here dwell children, young in years yet ancient in grief, yearning for love and care but deprived of kinship, the warmth of a familial upbringing. These children grow untended, steering through the complexities of life by themselves, the guiding hands absent.

They spend their precious years in this refuge, not under natural care but rather perfunctory supervision, believing that their fairly basic orphanage is the closest thing to home. But as they arrive at the precipice of adulthood, their footsteps, once very eager to leave, falter, for the world outside beckons—an uncharted world fraught with uncertainty—and they must forge their own paths. There is no turning back.

The essentials of life, those fundamental necessities—not fancy, but essential: sustenance, clothing, and affection—remain inaccessible, flickering like will-o'-the-wisps just beyond their outstretched hands, and they are told, in words as cold as the winds of fate, that they are now on their own, sovereigns of their destiny. Yet a truth haunts their hearts: have they not always been thus?

Within the confines of this establishment lives a boy, isolated in a dormitory, named Clover Nelson. At just eight months old, his biological parents abandoned him at the doorstep of Whispering Hearts, an orphanage situated in the charming city of Nelson. From that moment, it became his only home.

Clover enjoys living in Nelson—not specifically the orphanage itself—because the city granted him the proud name of Nelson, making him the sole bearer of this surname among the ninety-two children. Most arriving at the orphanage had surnames, but Clover did not until then. Perhaps his parents forgot to mention it in the letter, prompting Agatha Preen, the head of the orphanage, to append Nelson to his name. Clover feels special. But the specialty falls short when it comes to his form. He is a small and frail boy who appears two years younger than his chronological age, solely due to malnutrition.

Whispering Hearts is a two-story building with thirty rooms. A dormitory typically houses four children, but Clover has a room to himself, a rarity in such settings. But he does not resent this; he believes he is privileged, while other children envy him for it.

At times, he feels lonely when life beyond the walls reaches his ears—the laughter, the chatter, the bursts of discord from neighboring rooms—evoking the craving to partake. Yet the other children exclude him, and he often wonders if it's out of jealousy or hatred.

From the window, he peers outside, his chin cradled in his palms, his elbows resting on the window ledge. Earth has completed eight trips around the sun since he entered the alchemy of time, a child of the summer who drew his first breath in the balmy comfort of June 1991. Born with the spirit—a shard of summer itself—his voice is as melodious as a songbird, his demeanor calm and serene like the stillness of a clear, starlit June night.

His parents would be proud of him, if only they were present. Nevertheless, Clover has managed to instill in himself the essential qualities of kindness and civility. Still, he occasionally thinks about his parents, unaware of who they are or where they might be, with no pictures to remind him.

As he gazes at his faint reflection in the grimy window, he wonders if he resembles them. Maybe his deep brown eyes are like his mother's, or his large ears are a lineament from his father. But he may only wonder, for he is benighted about his origins, as were the tribes.

Nelson is a laid-back yet enchanting place where art and culture thrive. Though it mingles harmoniously with nature, it upholds its city-like vibrancy. Each historical building represents a tale from the past, from quaint cottages to Gothic-inspired monuments, with numerous galleries and boutiques blooming like wildflowers throughout the city.

Yet the true heart of Nelson lies in its natural beauty, where mountains rise and glacial lakes reflect the azure skies. The majestic peaks of the Selkirk enclose the city. The waters of Kootenay Lake are cool and deep. When rain descends, the mountains blur like a distorted dream. This verdant wilderness, with its indescribable allure, attracts tourists from all corners of the globe, eager for adventure and mirth. Here, kayakers glide across crystal-clear streams.

It is a haven for wildlife: ospreys dive into the water for fish, while eagles soar against breathtaking sunsets. Squirrels dart between branches, dancing in the treetops, while bears lumber through nearby forests and cougars prowl the rugged terrain. Deer and other wildlife occasionally emerge to quench their thirst, where waters kiss the shores.

Clover's curious eyes are fixed on the raindrops tapping against the window. A smile spreads across his face, causing his cheeks to rise like a blooming rose. He has been waiting since morning for the clouds to release the water condensed within them, and now that moment has arrived.

The windowpane fogs up, reminiscent of the distant grand summits. Clover's breaths create mist upon the glass, and he wipes it away with the back of his sleeve to look at the lively streets below.

"Umbrellas," he whispers in awe.

The cobbled streets shimmer, as umbrellas of various colors unfurl against the gray sky. People walk hurriedly, their footsteps blending with the falling rain. Clover inhales deeply and closes his eyes.

"I'm coming to you, Lake Fairy."

He rushes out of his small dorm, heading toward Agatha Preen's office on the ground floor.

He knocks gently.

"Come in," calls a raspy female voice.

Upon entering, he sees Agatha Preen, engrossed in a mug of cocoa. The redolence of the brew entices him, stimulating his salivary senses. Soon, he finds his mouth full of salivary secretions. He swallows hard and approaches her desk.

Clover and the other children are not allowed to have hot cocoa until Christmas. It is August, and he begins counting the months until winter. *August ... September ... December*, he thinks, then remembers, *Oh, I forgot November.* Unfolding his fingers, he calculates that three months remain.

Agatha remains focused on the papers on her desk, not yet acknowledging him. Clover's gaze falls on the mug of hot cocoa positioned atop an electric warmer, with wisps of steam rising from it. *How warm and delicious it must taste*, he thinks.

He often wonders why hot cocoa is reserved solely for winter months, a rule strictly applied to the children, while adults like Agatha enjoy it at will. Clover finds this odd but refrains from protesting, even though hot cocoa is his favorite.

"You?" Agatha finally looks up from her paperwork. "What is it?" she asks, her hands tapping on the wooden table. "Why can't you just stay in your room?"

"Er..." Clover fidgets with his hands, nervousness gripping him, but he gathers the courage to say, "I want to ask for your permission."

Agatha rolls her droopy eyes and sighs. A gust of wind loosens her bun, causing her auburn hair to cascade down her shoulders as she ties it back into a low ponytail. "Are you asking to go to Kootenay Lake again?"

In tentative delight, Clover's lips form a jittery grin. "Y—yes."

Agatha leans back in her chair, fiddling with her pen. "Go then. You're eight," she says. "But you know the rules. Be careful."

"Thanks, Ms. Preen," Clover says, filled with joy.

He turns toward the door, but Agatha calls after him, "Just don't die, okay? Be sure to come back. You're starting school next month."

It's become a casual warning from Agatha, but Clover finds it awkward every time she says, *Just don't die.* He typically responds with a nod and silence, preferring not to engage in further conversation. With permission granted, he leaves, following his heart wherever it leads him.

However, he can't help but wonder if Agatha is genuinely concerned for him, as her way of expressing that concern feels inappropriate. Who says that to a child? But Clover does not judge or jump to conclusions. *Maybe she's just worried about me,* he tells himself, assuming something may have happened in her past. Despite everything, he believes she is kind enough to let him explore, whether on busy main roads or in the deep woods full of wildlife.

Clover also contemplates the second part of Agatha's statement: the start of his formal schooling next month, and the peculiarity of his delayed education. Although excited to finally go to school, he acknowledges the sheer anomaly of not having started earlier. The decision was Agatha's, and she chose not to send Clover when he turned five. The rationale behind this remains a mystery.

Clover has always had a bittersweet relationship with summer break. The upside is that he doesn't have to watch younger children leave for school. The downside is that those school-going children often consider themselves superior to him, taunting him daily. Summer break only prolongs the period during which Clover endures their cruel remarks for simply existing.

The permission is granted. Clover steps out of Agatha's office and makes his way to his dormitory. Once in his room, he carefully retrieves a jacket from his dilapidated closet, mindful not to overload the shelves that might collapse; they are predominantly empty, as his clothing is scant. Whatever he possesses is due to the generosity of local residents who often donate to the orphanage.

Donations come once a month, but the children cannot choose their items; Agatha distributes them. Clover rarely receives well-fitting clothes; they are often too small or too large. His current shoes, which he has had for two years, were once oversized but now fit snugly. Yet he cares little for the shoes he wears, as he has managed to get his hands on something the last time the box of donations came: a pair of the neatest-looking boots, nearly brand new.

He considers himself fortunate. These boots, which he keeps hidden from everyone, including himself, rest quietly beneath his bed, swathed in cling film to protect them from dust and blemish. Lowering his head, Clover bends down and gently pulls the boots out from under the bed.

"There you are," he whispers, breaking them free from their plastic coating. The boots may not be flawless, but they are perfect for Clover. He has never worn them, and today will be the ideal day to test their durability.

He examines the shoes closely, admiring their beauty from every angle, running his hands over the gleaming black leather, and, with careful attention, he inverts them to inspect every part.

At that moment, he spots what steals his heart's serenity—not merely one, but multiple cracks in the soles. A perplexed furrow settles on his brow; he is far from enthused by this discovery. Clover's spirits, which soared like an eagle moments ago, have plummeted.

"Oh no!" Tears well up in his eyes, and his chagrin is evident on his face. He had dreamed of taking a stroll around the lake in these very boots, but it seems they aren't waterproof.

Clover drops onto the floor with an emphatic plonk, hanging on to the boots tightly. His gaze shifts to the window, where water droplets still cling. It is still raining, he thinks, on the verge of abandoning his plans, but he cannot. So, with a heavy heart, he rises from the floor.

"I'll wear these boots," he declares. "There's nothing wrong with them. It's okay if my feet get a little wet."

It is a brave decision, but his insides curse him for having discarded his old boots upon acquiring these. While these boots are certainly fancier and sturdier than his previous pair, at least the old ones were functional; they had no cracks. He could walk in them in rain, snow, or sunshine without water seeping through.

But now Clover has no choice. He cannot gallivant outdoors in his current shoes, for they are weathered, his toes pushing against the fabric with no room to splay. With laces gone, they are inadequate; water may seep through the soles. Reluctantly, he removes his old shoes and dons the new pair.

They look splendid and fit him impeccably. He desires to like them, and indeed, he does. His only concern lies in their functionality.

Nevertheless, he remains optimistic, wishing himself luck as he exits the room and rushes down the staircase. Approaching the door, he pauses. A bin catches his eye, filled with overturned umbrellas. In need, he surveys them. No one is around—it's a great opportunity.

He sifts through each one until his hands settle on a distinctive pink umbrella decorated with black polka dots. He picks it up, ready to step outside.

"Where are you taking that brella?"

A girl, roughly ten, appears behind Clover, arms crossed and lips pouting. Flicking her brunette hair, she approaches him, her piercing green eyes filled with disdain. "Tell me."

Clover shakes his head. *Why did you have to show up?* he thinks. The prospect of running into someone is the last thing he fancies before going out. Never has anyone, particularly Rina, let him choose and pick anything for himself. The autonomy of choice is long extinguished. But Clover does not want to delay his plans, so he opens the door.

Feeling a need to correct her, he turns around. "It's called an umbrella, not a brella."

Rina narrows her eyes and flares her nostrils. "I'll call it brella because my friends at school call it brella."

"Well, you should tell them it's incorrect," Clover says, keeping his composure.

"You don't even go to school," Rina retorts, her lips puckering like a clown in a whimsical display. "How do you know what it's really called?"

Clover lets out a giggle. "You know, it doesn't take a genius to know this." He snorts. "Besides, I can read and write. You don't need to go to school to learn that."

Rina is out of valid retorts and says, "Okay, smarty pants. Now, put that back. It's mine."

Her tone radiates superiority, which Clover dislikes. "It's everyone's, Rina. Not just yours."

"Well, it's pink, and pink belongs to girls."

"No," Clover insists, gripping the umbrella tighter. "Said who? That's not right. Boys can like pink too."

Rina rolls her eyes, brushing away a few baby strands of hair from her face. "You like pink because you are half-boy."

Clover parts his lips, blood rushing to his ears. "Can you stop calling me that?" he shouts. "I'm a boy, and I can like pink."

"No, you cannot like pink." Rina flares her nostrils again, extending her hand. "It's for me. Now give it back."

Clover sighs, his patience wearing thin. "Listen," he says, with a trace of confidence, though his legs tremble. "I like this umbrella, so I'm taking it outside. Okay? I won't give it to you."

"You'll look like a fool," Rina groans, her cheeks flushing with frustration. "You know, walking around with that pink brella."

"I'm more than fine with looking like a fool," Clover says, spreading the umbrella and stepping out the door.

"I'm going to tell Rodney," Rina declares, a sly smirk forming on her lips. "I bet you won't like that."

Clover halts on the last step. Rodney is a bully, and the mere mention of his name fills Clover with dread. Rodney has beaten him up several times, often calling him a "girly boy." Clover despises him but cannot discern the reason behind his toxic conduct.

Perhaps it's Clover's fondness for "girly" things, like the color pink and stuffed dolls, but he also enjoys basketball. Yet he is excluded from playing with the other boys in residence, relegating him to solitary games in the backyard. Maybe it's not boyish enough for Rodney.

The color drains from Clover's face, and his insides twist. Slowly, he turns around and begins climbing the steps back to the door.

"Scared? I would be, too." Rina smirks, extending her hand again. "May I?"

The pink umbrella. How Clover wishes to walk beneath its vibrant canopy, but he knows it's unwise to defy Rina, for retaliation may follow. So he reluctantly relinquishes the umbrella, his desire, to her.

"Here," he says quietly.

Rina snatches the umbrella from him and tosses it in the bin. "Good."

"But I need an umbrella," Clover protests. "I'll get doused."

It's as if his words float around Rina, never quite landing lest they penetrate her mind. "Doused? What does that mean?"

Clover draws in a profound inhalation. "Soaked. I meant soaked."

Rina crosses her arms again, her stare tapering. "Who taught you that word? You've never been to school."

"That doesn't matter," Clover says. "I told you I read every day."

Rina dismisses him with a scoff. "Fine!" she exclaims, suddenly grabbing a weathered umbrella from the bin and thrusting it in his direction. Clover manages to catch it. "Bye," she says before slamming the door in his face.

Clover exhales a sigh carrying deep disappointment and heartache. He looks at the umbrella in his hand, a dull, lifeless brown, stripped of any cheer or color.

In a different life, one with his parents, he imagines having a vibrant collection of umbrellas, each for a different mood: sunny yellow, playful pink, calming blue, rich red, and lively green—but never black or brown. Yet his current circumstances have left him resigned to this faded, well-worn umbrella.

As he grips the handle and attempts to open it, every joint resists with a grating defiance. The ribs seem almost unwilling to unfold, and Clover battles with their rigidity. It's a struggle to pry it open, but with an assertive pull, he finally succeeds.

Clover lets out a soft whimper and thinks, *Why can't I have what I want? What's wrong with boys liking pink? Why are Rina and Rodney always after me?*

His mind spins with endless musings, thoughts branching off in all directions. But for now, he must set aside his dismay, because he is finally going to lay eyes on the person he longs to see most: his Lake Fairy.

Three

A STROLL THROUGH NELSON

The trek to the lake has always been a series of staccato escapades for Clover, dictated by the volitions of the Lake Fairy, who only calls him under the veil of rain or the cloak of snow; her call otherwise remains muted. So Clover waits with bated breath for the opportune meteorological alignment.

The duration of the journey, an unrushed saunter, takes a full hour but is no burdensome bane for him. Rather, it is a triviality, as his desire to be outside the orphanage outweighs the length of the walk.

That fine day has finally come. He stands at the crossing, ready to begin his voyage, but he looks up to find the rain has escalated from a mere drizzle. The pewter clouds loom overhead, bearing heavy tons that suggest an impending downpour. In line with predictions, the once mellowing rain transmutes into sporadic heavy drops that drum unabashedly against Clover's umbrella. While he enjoys the melody of rain tapping against the fabric, he is unsure if continuing his journey to the lake is wise.

The heavy caress of rain welcomes him. The umbrella shakes, and his small frame nearly disappears beneath it. The thundering clouds cause every hair on his body to stand on end. The umbrella struggles valiantly against the onslaught of rain, but the winds grow mightier, threatening to invert it—and Clover himself—a shield that has become a useless tangle of fabric and metal.

He grips the handle tightly, his knuckles turning white, determined to maintain this flimsy barrier between himself and the sky's aggressive blitz. The rain envelops Nelson like a curtain, blurring it in a blanket of gossamer gray. Cars and buses roar by, indifferent to the plight of pedestrians, and Clover is one of them.

He steps back from the curb each time a vehicle passes, avoiding the splashes of rainwater. Besides, his shoes are less than perfect. The pedestrian signal seems to take an eternity before it finally turns green. He must cross the street now or forever wait.

With one giant leap, he launches forward to cross the road. His heart flutters, and his eyes widen as he gauges the distance, eager to reach the other side. The inverse countdown begins: his small feet have three seconds to finish crossing, and with one last push, he succeeds.

Suddenly, a strong gust wrenches the umbrella from his grasp, sending it tumbling away to roll and flap pathetically on the wet asphalt. Clover watches it disappear, his heart sinking. Now completely exposed to the rain, he feels its full force—cold, unyielding, merciless.

He shivers and runs after the umbrella, but the capricious winds whisk it further away, forcing him to chase it again. Finally, it gets stuck against a bench. He reaches for it, heaves a sigh, and flings it over his head.

Useless now, he thinks. *I'm already drenched.*

Taking a deep breath, he squares his shoulders and steps back onto the sidewalk, focused on reaching somewhere dry for shelter.

Seeped in moisture from crown to sole, he pauses near an artisan gallery. The winds are powerful, and he shuts his umbrella, hoping the gallery's awning will provide some protection. But the rain's precision pierces through, and its relentless assault leaves his clothes clinging to his skin like a second layer. His hair, matted down, drips onto his forehead, sending tiny droplets splattering down his cheeks.

Clover opens his umbrella again, positioning it behind him while he turns his face toward the gallery. This offers some shield against the downpour, and although he is already bathed in weeping clouds, he wants to avoid being attacked by the ceaseless deluge from both streets and skies.

Shivering profoundly, he tries to distract his mind and glances through the misty window of the gallery. The vibrant art inside draws him into a world of wonder, and he hopes to find some relief from the damp chill wrapping around him. The gallery exudes warmth and offers shelter from the rain and the outside world.

As he gazes through the glass, Clover momentarily loses himself in colors and shapes, forgetting his soaked condition, his spirit briefly uplifted by the silent exchange between art and observer.

Though Clover lives across the street, he has never visited this gallery. He usually only passes by, offering a fleeting glance at the craftsmanship on display. But today, he has time to explore the artistry within.

Clover places the umbrella on the ground and opens the door. A soft chime rings out as his heart thumps against his ribcage, part of him anxious because he doesn't have any money with him. His pockets are devoid of currency, yet he has valiantly entered the crafter's hub.

What if an artistic marvel beckons him, pleading silently to be taken home, but he can't? What if his empty pockets render him powerless to answer its call?

As he enters the shop, he urges himself not to be swayed by anything fancy. He will wander the gallery until the rain slows down, then set forth.

Clover enters the shop timidly, his movements heavy with wet garments and squelching shoes. Looking back, he notices a trail of rainwater he leaves behind.

"Hello, dear boy," a male voice says.

Clover turns to find a middle-aged man with balding gray hair standing before him, his stark blue eyes riveted on Clover's drenched appearance.

Fear sings its cold song in his ears. He quivers and wraps his arms around himself, tucking away damp hair from his forehead, acutely aware of his state and bracing for a reprimand for tracking in the aftermath of the rain.

"Er... I—I am sorry, sir."

Clover twists and turns as if wringing himself dry, his mind conjuring scenarios of being scolded or asked to leave. But to his surprise, the man smiles. Clover squints at his name tag.

"Umm, Mr. James, I think I'll... just go."

"Never you mind, my dear," James says. "It's pouring, don't you see? Stay here."

Clover relaxes and smiles back at him. James keeps his hands tucked inside the pockets of his blue-and-white apron.

"Stay as long as you wish, but if you need anything, just call me, all right? Just don't touch anything."

"N—no!" Clover's voice chokes. "I won't. I'm not here to, you know, buy anything. I just came for shelter."

"Okay." James smiles again and retreats, leaving Clover to wander the gallery alone.

Inside, it is just him and James. Clover feels a surge of gratitude for being allowed to stay.

As he roams the shop, curiosity guides him through the labyrinth of artistic wonders. His fingers itch to trace the edges of hand-carved sculptures, to feel the convoluted grooves and curves. But he has been warned not to touch anything.

Clover sighs and steers toward the jewelry section, where his heart skips a beat. His eyes widen at the gleaming bijouterie arranged on a table. He leans over the display, captivated by the array of jewels.

The wooden cases resting on a luxurious red velvet substrate hold an assortment of metalworks and shiny gemstones—rings, earrings, bracelets, pendants, and a plethora of other ornamental treasures.

In sheer delight, Clover gazes upon a sea of jewels he has never seen before. He is awestruck, loves such finery, and dreams of rings with varied stones. Yet he cannot understand why he feels such fascination.

Smitten and mesmerized by the spectacle, his eyes admire every piece of ornament on the table. But then his gaze shifts toward a shiny treasure hidden among the others: a silver ring embellished with a resplendent sapphire.

Clover cannot help himself; his hands involuntarily reach for the ring. Though internal thoughts whisper to him, *Just don't touch anything,* a repetition of the caution James voiced not too long ago, his curiosity is too fierce to quell, urging him forward to lay his hands on the ring.

Gathering his courage, Clover picks up the ring, scrutinizing its beauty. A desire to own it ignites within him. However, a subdued reminder echoes in his mind: *You do not have the money for it. Put it down.*

But he just can't.

It is a stunning piece of jewelry, the sapphire as blue as the cosmos, fastidiously set into the silver ring, taking the elegant form of a swan, a complex masterpiece imbued with precision.

"Ah! So beautiful," Clover mutters, admiring the ring.

The truth dawns upon him: he cannot have the ring, even though he wants it with all his heart. It is beyond his reach.

With a deep sigh, he returns the ring to its casing and rummages through his sodden pockets, where he finds nothing—neither a trace of paper bill nor the clink of coinage. But it does not hurt him. He smiles, thinking it's nothing new; he has grown accustomed to adapting to fate's eccentricities.

There are many things he simply cannot have because his parents are absent. But he has never displayed a longing for material things—except for hot cocoa, which hardly qualifies as materialistic.

Still, a fervent desire to possess this ring lingers within him. He looks at the jewel's gleam. It lures him, but it remains a distant dream. His pockets are empty. Longing fills his eyes, a desire for unattainable splendor.

Frustration simmers within him, the sting of knowing he cannot possess it. Yet he is willing to give his fate a try.

He storms to the counter where James stands behind the cash register, busy cleaning a wooden ship with a microfiber cloth.

"Hello, sir."

"Yes?" James places the ship on the counter and lowers his head, staring into Clover's dark, beady eyes. "Found something?"

"Yes," Clover replies, clasping his hands behind his back. "If you will, please come along."

"Sure." James nods and steps out from behind the counter.

Clover leads him to the jewelry table and points at the sapphire ring. "How much for that ring?" His voice carries a hint of defeat. He is merely taking a chance. "I know it's very expensive, and—"

"It's not that expensive," James says.

Clover's face brightens as if the sun has kissed his soul. "Really?"

"Yes, only seventy-five dollars. It's not a real sapphire. If it were, I would've kept it under my nose, you know."

Once a radiant ray of dawn, Clover's smile fades into twilight. He isn't concerned about whether it's a real sapphire; the price is what troubles him, far too high for his budget. Seventy-five dollars? He wonders how much more a real sapphire would cost. Perhaps a genuine sapphire would be worth more than he is.

James notices Clover staring into the distance, quiet and deep in thought, and perhaps he understands the reason behind his silence. "Don't have enough for it?"

Clover shakes his head, his eyes downcast. "No, sir."

"Well," James lowers his head, resting his palms on his knees, "how much do you have with you right now?"

Clover hesitantly glances up, glimpsing James's eyes fall pitifully upon him. "Two dollars," he admits, bowing his head in shame for having entered an art gallery with only two dollars. *I'm either brave or stupid, or maybe both.*

He hears James let out a breath as he straightens his back, slightly frazzled but intrigued. "If you didn't have the money, why did you ask for its price?"

Clover feels as if the words have deserted him. He peers at James, unable to answer. His question is valid, but his presence here in the gallery feels out of place.

James crosses his arms, waiting for a response.

In a moment of clarity, confidence rekindles within him. "I may not afford it right now," he says, "but one day, I will."

Clover does not know why he says that. He thinks deeply about formulating means to amass the necessary funds for the ring, recalling how he previously earned money—never close to the price insignia of the ring —by assisting in Agatha's office, cleaning restrooms, mowing lawns, and running errands for the orphanage.

Agatha gives him a quarter for every completed task. If he continues to do more of these tasks regularly, he may accrue the requisite sum. Now, the path to transforming his desire into a tangible reality becomes clear to him.

James, eyebrows raised, studies Clover, contemplating his reply but offering no spoken words.

The silence stretches, and Clover feels compelled to break it. "The reason I asked the price, sir," he continues, "is to see if I can arrange the money. I wonder if you can please keep it for me until then."

"And again," James asks, "how will you arrange the money?"

An epiphany descends upon Clover. "I'll work for it, sir."

James gives a slight nod, perhaps impressed by Clover's determination. But Clover stands there, heart racing, uncertain if his request will be granted.

"So... will you?" Clover asks. "Please give me some time to sort it out, and I can tell you when I can pick up the ring."

James continues to observe Clover curiously. "Why do you want this ring? And most importantly, where are your parents?"

The familiar sinking feeling returns at the mention of his parents, as he must reveal, *I don't have parents.*

"I live across the road at Whispering Hearts Orphanage."

The man cups his mouth, feeling sorry for Clover. A slight squeal escapes his lips. "I'm so sorry, boy."

Clover offers a tight-lipped smile. "It's all right, sir," he says. "I'm okay."

"Are you really?" James asks, finding it bizarre that someone without parents could be fine.

"Yes, sir. I have a separate dorm. No one else in the orphanage has that. I don't have to share my space with anyone," Clover explains, a hint of pride in his voice. "Ms. Preen is very kind and gives me special treatment. She even gave me my surname."

"Oh! Agatha Preen?"

"Yes."

James falls silent, puzzled by Clover's praise for her. To his knowledge, goodness finds no fertile ground in her heart. Everyone knows she is an alcoholic, and he recalls her causing a ruckus on the streets in her younger years. Besides, she hates children. *How can she be so merciful toward this boy?* he thinks. *Maybe time has really changed her, and she has become a different person. Who can tell?*

"Sir?" Clover interrupts James's thoughts.

James blinks, returning from his reverie. "What's your name, boy?"

"Clover Nelson," he responds with a grin. "Please tell me if you can set the ring aside for me."

"Tell me, Clover," James says. "What will you do with this ring? Your fingers are"—he traces Clover's hands with his own—"tiny. This ring is too big for you."

"I'm not buying it for myself."

"Then, for whom is it?"

"My Lake Fairy," Clover replies.

"A fairy?" James snorts, finding the situation hilarious. "Sure, Clover."

Clover arches his brows, unsure why James is laughing at the mention of his fairy friend. "She is real, sir."

James stops and clears his throat. "Of course, she is."

"Yes, she is a very nice woman. She teaches me math and English. She sings with me, too, and we dance together along the lakeshore."

James looks perplexed and believes this Lake Fairy is merely a figment of Clover's imagination. Though there is a lake nearby, surely no fairies live around.

"Okay," he says to Clover, "you may take the ring and give it to your Lake Fairy."

"Sorry?" Clover is taken aback. He distrusts his fate and is confused. "But I don't have the money for it now."

"You can pay me later," James says, gathering the ring from the table. "Have it."

He shuts the casing and hands it to Clover.

Clover secures the ring in his pocket, thanking him. "I'll pay you, sir," he promises. "Soon."

James smiles and glances outside. "I think you should leave, maybe go back home to change. Okay?"

Clover peers out the window, noticing the rain ease to a gentle drizzle —not vast, yet enough. He isn't as deterred as before, and his clothes have dried a bit.

James ushers him outside, and with his umbrella overhead, Clover steps onto the streets of Nelson. He does not reason with changing his clothes for the journey ahead, trusting the air will dry them soon.

He ventures on, past the museums, where he sees a smattering of people seeking refuge beneath the canopies of local shops. Still, many are out and about, birling their colorful umbrellas while tourists flit from one shop to another.

Despite the recent tumultuous weather, Nelson continues its lively dance in the drizzle. The streetlights, embellished with a shimmering luster from the rain, bathe the streets in a soft glow.

As Clover continues his journey, he notices children reveling in the delight of puddles. He stops to watch them, drawn not to the puddles or their laughter but to the tall, colorful rain boots they wear—fancy and capable of keeping the water out.

For a moment, he thinks of joining them but quickly remembers the cracks in his own boots. Jumping in puddles would only make them worse. Besides, he can already feel the water seeping into his socks.

The children wear raincoats in vibrant yellow. Clover leans against a lamppost, watching their laughter and carefree antics, with no one to stop them from enjoying themselves. They laugh and play, while mothers call from balconies, summoning the children home.

How beautiful it is to be awaited by someone. That's how a child's life should be. That's how my life should be.

Continuing on, Clover strolls past bakery shops, enticed by the sweet scent of cinnamon wafting through the air, beckoning him to indulge in the irresistible treats.

Maybe I can buy a cinnamon roll. I have some money, he thinks.

Rummaging in the inner pocket of his coat, he retrieves a single two-dollar coin, his only possession of wealth at that moment. Before him is Madeline Treats, where each cinnamon roll costs seventy-five cents, tax included.

If he makes the purchase, he'll be left with just a dollar and a quarter —not much, perhaps enough for another cinnamon roll, and that's it. He wonders if it's truly worth spending all he has on a treat that will vanish in his stomach in under a minute.

Ms. Madeline is a kind woman. He remembers that whenever he visits her with a handful of coins—never more than four dollars—she often doesn't take any money from him. It could be pity or simply her generosity toward everyone.

However, he isn't seeking a free cinnamon roll today. He's already received a ring from James, which is enough favors for one day.

As he walks down the eclectic storefronts and cozy cafés, the path widens and unfolds into a scenic route. The quaint shops are replaced by tall trees adorned with raindrops. Occasionally, a substantial droplet breaks free from the leaves, tapping gently on Clover's umbrella.

Clover nears the lake, where the mist thickens. He walks confidently, undeterred. Avoiding the typical tourist trails, he diverges, tracing the wooded shores where twigs and broken branches litter the ground.

Clover closes his umbrella and leaps over the rocks, excitement coursing through him. He is exactly where he is meant to be.

As he goes deeper into the woods, a dreamy, forgotten land where fairies dwell, he calls out, "Lake Fairy!"

Four

THE ORPHAN AND THE OUTCAST

"Lake Fairy!" Clover calls again. "Where are you?"

He moves through dense groves and beneath ancient shoots, but his calls go unanswered, absorbed by the thicket. Desperation creeps into his voice as he scans each dark corner, but she remains like mist, ever untouchable, seemingly faded into the forest's mystique, leaving him to wander through the dim woods.

He wonders where he will find her in the heart of the rain-kissed woodlands. *Where should I go? It usually doesn't take this long for her to appear. What a strange turn this afternoon is taking.*

Exhausted from his fruitless search, Clover begins to return to the lake. As he flits through the forest, he spots a rock—a perch to alleviate his weariness—and settles upon it, still thinking of the Lake Fairy, disheartened and tired.

Let me try one more time, he thinks.

So, he yells. He cries out. His heart drums against his ribs. Breaths quicken; shivers crawl down his spine; hope wanes, but still, his fairy friend is not in sight. The forest is eerily quiet; the only sound is the soft rain murmuring through the leaves.

It seems futile to wait any longer, so he stands to leave, but his eyes still dart through the misty air, seeking a shadow or a sign. It feels as though she has decided not to show up for Clover today.

"I'm here," a voice suddenly pierces the haunting impassivity.

Clover stops in his tracks and breathes a sigh of reassurance. His fairy friend has declared her presence, and she will reveal herself any moment now.

"My dear Clover," a soothing voice calls to him from behind. "Turn around," she whispers.

Clover spins around to find his Lake Fairy, a goddess-like woman with pulchritudinous grace and a divine smile. "Finally!" he exclaims, flinging his arms around her legs.

She is as tall as a towering oak, a fairy of ebony hues, drinking light around her. Her eyes are portals to another world: crimson; no specks of melanin exist. She is a paradoxical blend of eerie charisma and haunting beauty, yet Clover feels no fear. His love for his fairy friend grows exponentially every time the sonnet composed by destiny brings them together like verses.

"What took you so long?"

The fairy kneels, fluttering her tendril-like lashes, each blink capable of mesmerizing him.

"It was raining so hard," Clover says, crossing his arms and pouting.

The Lake Fairy beams, her smile radiant and adding to her ethereal beauty. "Isn't that a good thing?" she asks. "We must only meet when it rains; when it shines, we must retreat to our safe haven."

"But why?" Clover sighs in exasperation. He longs to see her every day. "Why must you hide when it shines?"

"Because ordinary people must not see me," she explains, rising and circling a tree. "I'm an outcast."

Her nonchalant admission is something Clover has heard many times.

"I don't understand why you're an outcast," Clover says, perhaps for the hundredth time. "You're the nicest person I've ever known."

"My dear Clover," she says, "it's because my spirit pirouettes to a different beat."

She glides through the forest, leaping from bough to bough.

Clover pivots on his heels, following his fairy's leaps, feeling both mesmerized and confused. "What do you mean?"

The Lake Fairy stops twirling and, with a rhythmic walk, approaches Clover, who looks bewildered. "I'm different," she states, gazing into his confused eyes.

Clover blinks, thinking, *How is she any different?* But a voice takes flight from his seat of emotions to his orator. "Because you're nice," he says. "Yes, you're different because you're kind, unlike others."

And it's a soothing verity; she is indeed kind to Clover, unlike his mother, his father, Rodney, and Rina.

"You're kind too, my dear," the fairy says, leaning closer, "nice and different."

Clover shrugs, his skin prickling. Her breath smells of meadows kissed by dew. He gulps and follows her out of the woods toward the lake.

"Lake Fairy?" he asks, taking lumbering steps behind her. "You took a long time to show up today. Were you busy?"

The fairy twirls elegantly, maintaining her reverse path with bewitching elegance. "I had some rituals to complete," she says.

"What is a ritual?" Clover asks, his eyebrows knitted like a tangled maze.

The fairy chuckles at his innocent inquiry. "A task, my dear, that can only be done when the skies weep."

"I don't understand." Clover continues to stare at her as they walk.

She giggles, turns around, and declares, "I'm a witch, my dear Clover. I delve into the arcane, perform rituals, and other witchy works."

"I know you do magic," Clover says. "But—witchy works? What is that?"

"Witchcraft," she explains. "It holds the mysteries of ancient times, the dignity of Mother Earth, and the allure of the cosmos. In the moon's glow, I conjure and create. In the rain, I let go and surrender, and in the snow, I brew potions of the essence of winter."

She stops and looks at Clover with a serene smile. "I'm no fairy." She flashes her pearly teeth again, flailing her arms. "See, I have no wings."

Clover doesn't understand any of it—her mention of rituals, her explanation of witchcraft, nothing at all. Her entire presence is, in fact, a riddle.

"You're a fairy, not a witch," he says.

The lake comes into view. The Lake Fairy cuts through the mist surrounding the lake and sits on a large rock, her temporary throne.

"I won't protest, my dear. Call me whatever you like." She grins.

Clover finds a small rock large enough for his little bottom. A question he has been eager to ask is at the tip of his tongue.

"When will you take me to your house, Lake Fairy? You live under the lake but have never taken me to your place. I want to see what it looks like."

The fairy glances at the crystal lake. "Not you, my dear. Never you."

"Why? I've asked you many times, but you never agreed," he says.

Clover is enthralled and wishes to visit her abode, wondering what mysteries her home might hold.

"Because my home is not a place for the likes of you; it is meant only for those who have strayed from the path—the bad children, and not just children, but all who have assumed their darker sides. I take them along with me."

"I don't get it." Still, he asks, "Why not me?"

The fairy stands and walks along the shore. "I only take those who in the darkness bask; to punish them is my task. Yours is a heart untouched, unmarred. In my territory, you'd find it hard. With an innocent spirit like a mouse, you will find no room within the walls of my house."

Clover fails to grasp it, his mind fogged by the puzzling rhyme of her words. "But can you not show me? From afar? I won't go inside."

The Lake Fairy sways her hand and calls him over. "Come here, dear boy."

Clover leaps toward her, and the fairy clasps his hand, guiding him to the shore, where the remarkably clear waters reveal a striking sight beneath the surface.

"Look over there," she gestures. "That's my house."

Submerged timber lies in the water, though it propounds a bare supposition whether the lumber she points to truly resembles a house.

Clover examines the submerged wood, trying to reconcile the fairy's claim that it's her house. His curiosity piques, and his mind goes into a ponderous descent.

"Is that really a house?" he asks, narrowing his eyes.

"Umm-hmm," the fairy says. "Only I can live under the lake."

Clover whips his head toward her. "The people you took down there," he quaffs his saliva, "how do they breathe? I don't think we can breathe underwater."

The fairy smiles. "They need not breathe. But you, my dear, don't worry. I'll never take you down there."

"Is that because I'm good?"

"Precisely! You're a good boy, Clover. I like you."

"I like you too, Lake Fairy."

The Lake Fairy enfolds him, sharing her warmth with his frail body.

Then it dawns on Clover—he has completely forgotten about the ring he obtained from James to give to his fairy friend. It's time to reveal it to her, but he hesitates, not because he doesn't want to give it to her, but because his soul carries the weight of this purchase.

He promised to requite James's kindness with the gold of the mortal realm; seventy-five dollars is the cost—not much, but still something he will work hard for a long time to earn.

He feels his pocket. The ring is there. His heart dances with joy as he takes out the casing and presents it to the fairy. "I got you something."

"What is it?"

The fairy crouches down and looks at the casing in Clover's tiny hands. Her palms slowly cup the box, her long, black-painted nails tracing its edges. She snaps it open, revealing the beautiful gem within.

A breathless gasp escapes her lips as she discovers a sapphire ring set in a silvery wreath, a swan carved upon it, polished like the moon—so beautiful that it overwhelms her with its brilliance.

"Clover, my dear. How did you get this?"

She rotates the ring between her fingers, astonished by the small boy before her. How did he manage to spend a fortune on this ring? Then she thinks, *he's an orphan. He has no fortune.* "Tell me, Clover," she asks.

"I bought it," Clover says with pride, elated beyond measure.

"How did you get the money for it?" the fairy asks, her tone becoming motherly and strict, which Clover doesn't mind.

"I'll work for the ring. I asked the gallery owner to keep it for me until I arrange the money," Clover continues, "but he told me to take it and pay him later."

The fairy admires the ring but keeps it back in the casing, thinking it's wrong to accept such a gift. "How much was it?"

"Don't worry—"

"How much was it?" the fairy speaks with assertion.

Clover bows his head. "Seventy-five."

The fairy gasps, sinks to the ground, and tells him, "That's too much."

"It's not," Clover says, folding his hands. "It's not real sapphire, you know. It's a fake."

"I know, my dear," the fairy says in a calm voice, "but there was no need."

Clover sighs and hunches his shoulders. "Please accept it, Lake Fairy. Please. I want you to wear it. I've never given anything to you—to anyone."

His harmless pleas work their magic, and the fairy retrieves the ring from its casing, slipping it onto her forefinger. The ring glides on effortlessly, as though it were destined to find its rightful digit.

"Thank you, Clover."

But I'll ensure you have the money to pay the owner soon, she thinks.

Clover's cheeks bloom as he observes the ethereal charm the ring bestows upon his fairy friend, enhancing her innate beauty. Pride swells within his chest—a rare sensation—having bought something for someone he adores, a feeling that fills him with immense dignity and joy.

"My dear," the fairy says, noticing his squeaky new boots. "Look at those boots."

Clover stares at his boots, once a source of joy when leaving the orphanage, but now ill-equipped for the rain. They betray their purpose, providing no shelter from the elements. Dewy socks and chilled feet bear witness to their inadequate protection; water seeps through the cracks, failing their fundamental role. His smile fades into disappointment.

"Are they new?" the fairy asks, excited that Clover is finally wearing something brand new, against the grain of his fate.

"No," Clover says sadly.

"Oh! But they look fine and untouched," she says.

"They are used." Clover turns away. "I thought they were good, but they have cracks in their soles."

The fairy senses the blues in Clover's words, the weight hidden behind his voice about his nonfunctional shoes. "I can mend them for you," she says, patting his shoulders. "Don't worry."

With a scintilla of hope in his eyes, Clover quickly slips off his shoes, showing their undersides to the fairy. "See, right here." He points to the unmistakable cracks for her inspection.

The fairy smiles and takes the shoes. "I'll be back," she says, then heads toward the forest.

Clover waits, anticipating his fairy friend's return. He removes his damp socks, letting them air in the misty aftermath. Rain's retreat leaves dew lingering. How might socks dry? He slips them back on, idly toying with pebbles by the shore.

The fairy reappears, bringing his footwear. Her face radiates a triumphant smile, suggesting successful restoration. Sitting beside Clover, she displays the repaired shoes with a flourish. "Here you go! All fixed," she announces, offering them back.

Gone without a vestige, the cracks have vanished completely. Clover leaps in euphoria, exclaiming, "How did you fix them?"

Amid Clover's ecstatic leaps, the fairy beams. "Deep in the woods is a tree that yields a magical substance," she explains. "An adhesive that can mend things in a jiffy."

Clover dons the repaired shoes, bounding to the lake's shallow edge to test their integrity against the water. To his delight, no seepage occurs, leaving his socks as moist as before—neither more nor less. Overjoyed, he wraps his fairy friend in a jubilant hug. "Thank you, Lake Fairy," he says, teeming with happiness.

They stroll along the lakeshore, a merry duo in harmony, reveling in each other's company.

"So, tell me, Lake Fairy, why don't you live in the city?"

The fairy's ebony gown gathers pebbles and droplets of water along the way. "I'm different," she remarks, "different from the norm."

"You look different, and that's all," Clover says. "But why live here?"

The fairy stops and bends down, fixing her gaze on Clover. "Look at my eyes," she says, widening her pupils. "I have red eyes. Red isn't common."

"They are beautiful," Clover says, blinking slowly. They are mesmerizing, without a doubt.

The fairy chuckles. "Indeed. But people think they are evil. Only devil-worshippers are born with red eyes."

"No, they aren't," Clover protests.

The fairy inhales deeply. "I'm a witch, an evil witch who does bad things to people." She glances at Clover, who has his mouth open. "Umm, that's what they say about me."

Clover eases his breath, then asks, "Do the people who blame you force you to live here?"

The fairy flips her long, straight hair to the side. "No, I left because I had to. I couldn't fit in. Now, the woods are my playground, and the lake is my home."

Clover leaps over a log. "Will you ever go back?"

"Maybe. But for now, I don't want to mingle in a society where people like you and me are neglected. I don't fancy living in misery."

Clover stops walking. "What exactly is misery? Do I live in misery?"

The Lake Fairy continues walking ahead, though she hears him. "Misery is a state of discomfort, displeasure, and disharmony. When you're unhappy and uncomfortable in your space, you're miserable. When you're deprived of basic human rights, you're miserable. When the air you breathe becomes suffocating, you're miserable. You are"—she whirls around—"miserable, Clover. There is nothing good about your state or your place. A very basic life you have, nothing to be proud of, nothing to be happy about."

He struggles to comprehend, thinking he is happy as he wears a mask of contentment, unaware of the misery that envelops his life. He views his existence through the lens of naïveté, finding joy in the smallest things, shaped by the narrow boundaries of his world—a life limited by the walls of the orphanage.

He has not tasted the sweetness of parental love nor experienced the freedom and abundance that lie beyond his known world. Yet Clover is unaware of the sorrow of his circumstance, so he ponders why the fairy claims his life qualifies as miserable.

"I have been okay, Lake Fairy. You should come to live there."

The fairy lifts Clover into her arms, as he is featherlight. "I know, my dear. But I cannot."

"Then let me come to live with you."

Her blood-red lips curve into a smile. "When you're a little older, you may live with me. But for now, I don't want you to." She sets him down.

"Why is that?" Clover continues to inquire. "Why do I have to wait until I'm older? What if I'm not here? What if I—I stop, umm, living?"

The fairy gasps, shocked and appalled by his words. "Don't you ever say that, okay? You've got a long way to go. You haven't even begun living, my dear."

"Okay, sorry," Clover says, bowing his head, unsure why he blurted it out.

He continues walking along the shore behind his fairy friend, but soon his steps begin to slow, and fatigue sets in. He gives up and sits down. "I don't think I can walk any further. I'm tired."

The fairy lifts him once more, and Clover's head rests against her shoulder, his eyelids growing heavy. "Sleep, my dear," she whispers, settling onto the ground with Clover's head nestled in her lap.

As evening descends, the sky transforms into a canvas of deepening hues, the last light of day casting a soft, glowing ambiance over the surroundings. The world around the lake becomes luminescent, where the lines between day and night begin to blur.

The lake's surface mirrors the evening tide, and Clover sleeps peacefully in the fairy's lap, undisturbed by the quiet arrival of dusk. With a gentle touch akin to a mother's, the fairy pats his head, wishing for his fatigue to dissipate like fading traces of a dream.

Clover stirs from his slumber, his eyes fluttering open to a breathtaking sight: a deer, draped in rare flaxen, sipping from the lake. The creature's elegance is accentuated by the soft evening light.

"Wow, that's so pretty," he whispers in awe, still in the fairy's lap.

"Isn't it?" the fairy says, gently setting him down on the ground beside her.

Clover's gaze remains fixed on the unusual deer. With a twist of her hand, the fairy seems to summon the creature closer. The deer responds to her call, approaching with soft, slow steps before bowing and resting its head in her lap.

The fairy strokes its head affectionately, leaning down to plant a kiss on its forehead. "It's my friend," she tells Clover, who watches with wide-eyed fascination. "All the creatures of the forest are my friends. I share a deep connection with nature, an extraordinary bond."

She glances up at the sky and then back at Clover. "You must leave now, my dear, before nightfall."

The fairy remains seated, her hands caressing the deer's face as it relaxes in her lap.

Clover looks skyward. The fairy is correct; the gloaming is waning. It's time for him to go. "Goodbye, Lake Fairy. We'll meet again soon."

With one last look at the enchanting scene before him, Clover begins his journey back, stepping onto the trail that leads toward the city, each step taking him further from the magical world of the fairy and her woodland companions and closer to the familiar sights and sounds of the city.

Soon, he will return to the reality of life in the orphanage, a life far removed from the mystical wonders he just experienced with his fairy friend.

Five

CAUGHT IN THE WEB

"Clover!"

Agatha Preen stands in the doorway, her gaze intense as a turbulent sea, arms crossed and nostrils flaring like a disdainful gust of wind.

"You're late," she says, tapping her foot impatiently.

Clover, breathless, has just returned to the orphanage. His little walk has taken longer than he intended, and now he must face the consequences.

"I—I'm sorry." He stumbles over his words, his head hanging low. "I didn't realize it was so late."

"Look up," Agatha commands. "And tell me what you see."

Clover looks up, uncertain of what to say. The sky is tar-black, punctuated by lavender patches, devoid of celestial asters—just a dull welkin that has just concluded spattering Nelson.

"Er... the sky?" he mumbles.

Agatha rolls her eyes and shakes her head, wearied by the inane conversation. "Stupid boy."

She holds his wrist tightly, pulling him inside, her grip firm enough to leave red imprints. Clover barely resists, flowing with her pull like a current in a stream, head down, wordless, and prepared to face the stern decree.

She leads him upstairs, her heels clicking sharply on the steps—click-click, click-clack—until they reach the second floor, where she hurls him into the room. "Stay here."

Clover falls to the floor as the door slams shut behind him. He remains there, tired of the way he is treated, unsure if he will even be allowed to eat now. His tardiness is evident; punishment is inevitable.

With a low, guttural noise escaping his throat, he tilts his head, scanning the uneven floor of his room, where a fine patina of dust covers the boards marked with countless scratches. The neglected corners are cloaked in grime. Continuing his survey, he slowly swivels his head to the right, still focused on the ground beneath him, peering under the bed, where the dust accumulates even more densely than in the rest of the room.

The grainy dirt clings to Clover's face, and just as he prepares to get up, he catches a ghastly sight. From behind the bed leg, a creepy eight-legged creature emerges, crawling toward him.

"Spider!" he screams, leaping off the floor and onto the bed, pulling his knees to his chest as he silently prays for the creature to disappear.

The spider pays no heed and continues its slow journey toward its new roommate, moving at a steady pace. Clover screams again, paralyzed with fear and unsure of what to do. The tiny arachnid reaches the edge of the bed.

Frozen with terror, his heart races wildly. He flinches, retreating to the farthest corner of his bed, his breaths quick and muffled. "Go away," he pleads, wishing the spider could understand, but it moves closer.

In a frantic bid to escape the looming encounter, he jumps from the bed and races toward the door in a panicked flurry. A shiver of horror courses through him. The room is locked. Agatha locked it after throwing him inside as punishment.

Now he is trapped in the room, with a spider.

He glances at the spider from the corner of his eye. It scuttles across the bed as if it belongs there, and no boy named Clover can reclaim it from the orb-weaver. The spider changes its pace, leaping to the ground, heading straight for Clover.

He turns toward the door and pounds on it. His cries for help are loud, but no one responds. Too desperate to flee, shivers wrack his panicking body.

The spider inches closer to Clover's toes. Now, he can no longer scream. Exhaustion overwhelms him. His legs give way beneath him, and his cries fade into muted sobs.

Collapsing against the locked door, his heart races with the terror of the unknown, his spirit drained by the overwhelming ordeal.

And then he becomes taciturn.

The silence of his despair dissolves his surroundings into darkness. The boy, terrified of spiders, lies on the ground, defeated in a maze of fear and distress.

* * *

In the hospital, the stench of rubbing alcohol tickles the nostrils, the continuous beeping of monitors increases trepidation, the incessant calls make hearts drop, and the low murmurs of staff flitting about with files in their hands and stethoscopes around their necks offer hope to the ailing.

In one of the wards, obscured by a thick green curtain, lies Clover, languid on the bed, yawning and eager to leave. "I'm so bored," he says.

It has been over a day since he was brought to the hospital in an ambulance. He fainted—literally fainted—from fear. He feels ashamed. Agatha is also not pleased and is currently being interrogated by the medical staff. The paramedics asked questions first, and now the hospital staff is doing the same. Clover doesn't understand why.

The nurse took Clover's statement when he was groggy, but he can barely remember what he told her. He assumes it must have been bad enough to get Agatha into trouble.

He jumps out of bed and peeks through the curtain. Some nurses are typing on their computers, some are on calls, and others are wandering in the lobby. But his nurse isn't around—the one who took his statement. He doesn't recall her face; he only remembers her voice. It was sweet and motherly. He'll know when she comes back.

Clover sighs and sprawls back on the bed, his eyes darting around the white walls. He is attached to a monitor, electrodes sticking to his body.

The fluctuating waves of the ECG monitor catch his attention. He holds his breath momentarily, watching the line remain unchanged.

He exhales, and nothing happens. Now he holds his breath longer, fascinated to see if the line flickers. It does, slightly. He pushes himself to hold his breath even longer, turning purple with every second, determined to see the line move. The numbers on the screen change, but the line continues its rhythmic waves, with only slight variations in the troughs and crests. Finally, he gives up with a large exhale and resumes normal breathing. The monitor continues to beep.

He lies back on the bed, staring at the ceiling, which is as quiet and still as the walls, offering no distraction from the tedium. He feels trapped in this state of boredom for what seems like an eternity. He wishes for something to do, but it's a hospital ward—what entertainment can it possibly offer?

There's a teddy bear on the chair beside his bed. The nurse gave it to him yesterday, but he has grown tired of playing with it. He wants to sleep, but a pounding headache thwarts his attempts.

Clover gets up again and walks outside the ward to the nursing station, wheeling his medical apparatus along. "Nurse!"

The nurse working on the computer tilts her head. She has a phone pressed to her ear and communicates with him through gestures. Clover makes a fist and taps his head, indicating his source of pain. The nurse grins and puts the phone down. "I'll get to you in a minute."

"Okay." Clover retreats to his ward, positioning the apparatus near the bed, and waits patiently for the nurse to see him.

The wait isn't long. The nurse arrives with his file. "Okay, Clover. What's the issue?"

"I have a headache, a bad one," he says. "Can you give me some medicine?"

The nurse lowers her spectacles to examine his patient chart carefully. "I see," she says, her voice barely rising above a whisper. "Let me check with Dr. Vasquez."

With that, she draws the curtain and departs.

Clover lies back down, forcing his eyes shut, but the spooky wrath of the spider replays in his mind. Ever since he was brought to the hospital, he has struggled with the trauma. Every time he closes his eyes, he sees the spider emerging from the shadows—the very same one from his last encounter, indelibly imprinted in his memory.

He recalls every detail: its size, its dark, segmented body, the way it skittered across the floor toward him, and his own reaction—his rigid body, collapsing in fear. His heart begins to beat faster as he tries to repel the image from his mind, but the more he tries to forget, the more vividly the spider appears. He snaps his eyes open, beads of sweat forming on his upper lip.

The nurse has returned, and Clover is grateful for her presence, unable to bear the throbbing pain any longer. She holds a syringe filled with red liquid.

"Do you prefer pills?" she asks.

"I've never had a pill before," Clover says. "Would it taste better than the liquid?"

The nurse stifles a laugh. "I can't say for sure, dear. But I think this one tastes better," she says, advancing with the syringe.

Clover opens his mouth, and the nurse administers the medicine. "There you go."

He enjoys the taste; his taste buds detect banana and cherry. He has never tasted cherry before, and he likes it. "Can I have more?" he asks.

The nurse spins around. "No," she says, shaking her head. "That's enough for the next six hours. It's medicine, not juice."

She leaves the ward, and Clover wonders if all medicines taste like cherry. He still savors the ambrosial potion lingering on his tongue. He reminisces about the times he fell sick at the orphanage, recalling how he was given different kinds of medicine—never cherry-flavored and never as delicious as this one.

After a while, the pain begins to fade, almost imperceptibly at first. His body relaxes, and he starts to feel better. However, the relief is short-lived. He hears a sound—Agatha's heels growing louder with each step.

Clover startles. *She is coming,* he thinks.

Agatha stands at the door, looking weary and defeated. "Come on, let's go," she says to Clover with a tempting sway of her palms.

Clover puts on his shoes but then hesitates. "Ms. Preen, these wires are still attached to me."

Agatha exhales sharply and lunges toward him. "Move over," she says, reaching to remove the electrodes herself.

"Wait!" a male voice warns.

A short man, presumably a doctor, enters the room, glaring at Agatha. "Who gave you permission to remove those?"

"I was given the green light to take him home." Agatha crosses her arms and looks away, muttering under her breath.

"Agatha Preen," the doctor says, carefully peeling the sticky patches from Clover's torso, "you'll be watched."

"What for?" Agatha asks, scoffing. "To care for children like Clover?"

"Yes," the doctor says quickly. He winks and smiles at Clover as he discards the last electrode patch into a nearby bin. Agatha's expression turns grim, and she stands with a demeanor exhibiting a serious pall. The doctor continues, "This is your first warning, and possibly your last. Locking children up and starving them is a crime. I want to stress that there will be consequences if it happens again."

"So what should I do?" Agatha's mouth twitches nervously, a forced smile appearing. "Let these little monsters make my life a living hell?"

The doctor does not respond.

"Clover went for a walk and came back so late that I got worried," she continues. "What if something had happened to him? Who would be responsible?"

"I understand," the doctor says. "But you should not have starved him."

"I merely delayed his meals. I locked him up to punish him," she insists. "And I opened the door an hour later. But... he was on the floor..." She pretends to weep, but no tears fall. It looks so insincere that the doctor nearly chuckles. "I was terrified. I brought him straight to the hospital. But now"—she looks up at the doctor—"I'm being treated like a criminal. How cruel!"

She pinches her forehead, emitting a squeal.

"Okay, Ms. Preen, you may go," the doctor says, extending his arm.

Agatha wipes away her invisible tears and grabs Clover by the arms. "Let's go, honey."

Clover stands frozen, as if struck by a thunderbolt from the blue.

Honey? That's an unusual term of endearment for him. "Huh?" he says, mouth agape.

The doctor observes Clover's reaction to Agatha. "What's wrong, Clover? Is everything all right?"

Clover nods, still transfixed by Agatha's penetrating gaze. "Yes, doctor."

Agatha forces another smile. "Come on, let's go home, Clover."

As they exit the ward, Clover follows Agatha through the hospital corridors, freshly discharged. He glances at the patient band on his wrist. *Nelson, Clover,* he reads, feeling butterflies in his stomach. He loves seeing his name; it reassures him that he exists.

He walks down the hall, where stretchers and wheelchairs pass by, their occupants looking as though all joy has been drained from them. He tries to smile at some, but only a young boy, about his age and holding a similar teddy bear, returns his grin.

Then it hits him: he forgot his teddy bear on the chair.

They reach the lobby, and Agatha inserts her parking ticket into a machine. Clover wants to ask about the teddy bear but hesitates, wondering if it even belonged to him. Maybe it has served its purpose, and now it is off to comfort another child like him.

Agatha and Clover hurry toward the parking lot outside the hospital. Clover fears her silence; he knows she can turn his life into a wretched hell. She sits in the car, and Clover takes the back seat. The door slams shut, and the engine roars to life as Agatha drives out of the hospital grounds.

Clover waits silently for the inevitable reprimand, but it doesn't come —yet.

They stop at a red light. Agatha slams the brakes, and the moment arrives. She turns her head toward the back, where Clover sits with his head lowered.

"You filth," she hisses, gritting her teeth but maintaining a calm tone. "Did you tell them I starved you?"

Clover lifts his head. "No, Ms. Preen," he says, nearly jumping out of his seat. "I told them I was late, and then you locked me up. I saw a spider in my room..." His lips form an *O* as he speaks, while Agatha's eyes narrow. "And then I—I don't remember anything after that." He lowers his head again.

The light turns green, and Agatha sets foot on the gas pedal. "Hmm."

Clover fears she is plotting another form of punishment. He knows he didn't accuse her of anything, but he feels powerless to persuade her otherwise. She is angry, ready to penalize him for telling the truth.

She drives into the orphanage through a back street, parking her car in one of the spaces. Clover scrambles to his feet as soon as she unlocks the door, eager to escape into the walls of his not-so-dear dwelling.

"Wait!" Agatha calls, and Clover freezes in place, paralyzed with fear. "Where are you running?"

Clover clasps his hands, fidgeting with his fingers, hesitant to turn around and face her.

"Turn around and look at me."

Heeding the call, Clover whirls around slowly.

Agatha, treading in doe-like strides, stops before Clover. "You don't dare mention anything that happened at the hospital to anyone here. Do you understand?"

Clover holds his breath. "Yes," he says, nodding blithely.

"Good." She exhales deeply, rubbing her forehead, looking visibly drained. "I wish you had never been born, Clover. I wish you hadn't ended up with me." Her voice sounds frayed.

Clover's heart skips a beat.

"But here you are," she continues, gazing skyward with her arms crossed, "abandoned by your parents, who never wanted you. But I took you in." She looks into his eyes, her tone brimming with disappointment. "And this is what I get in return."

Clover feels a weight of guilt for her plight, yet he cannot bring himself to apologize. He stands mute, looking at Agatha, whom he believes loves him, but her words feel anything but loving.

"You know," she says, "they will keep an eye on me because of you. Because of you, this orphanage will face regular inspections from care services. And do you know what will happen, Clover?"

Clover shakes his head.

A smirk curls on her thin lips. "You'll be taken away," she says. "You'll end up in a random foster home, and when they get sick of you, you'll pack your things into a black trash bag and move on to the next one, and then to another, until you turn eighteen. Then you're free—free to go wherever you like. Would you like that to happen?"

"No, please," Clover whispers.

The thought horrifies him: his life reduced to a transient existence, carried from one temporary home to another in a trash bag. He wonders if he will ever find stability, an anchor to hold onto. The prospect seems bleak, a grim reality he can't bear to face.

That would be a terrible fate for Clover. If only he had kept quiet.

Now he regrets his actions. Agatha did what she thought was right and punished him for being late. She was merely enforcing the rules. He blames himself for fainting, for his crippling fear of spiders, and now for his reckless confession to the nurse. Every word and action feels like a shovel digging his own grave.

"I'm so sorry," he says.

Agatha raises her forefinger. "For the time you're here, I want you to be silent—silent as if you didn't exist, silent as if you were never brought to this orphanage, silent as if you were dead."

Her eyes widen, tinged with red. "And this is your punishment."

Six

FIRST DAY OF SCHOOL

"Why can't it be morning already?" Clover mumbles, sitting by the window, eagerly awaiting the sunrise. It's only 5 a.m., and all he sees outside is the deep navy of the night sky, its celestial companions still suspended throughout the firmament, twinkling brilliantly in the darkest hour. Clover does not want to see the stars anymore, so he closes his eyes, wishing for the sun to rise and spill its golden light over the city.

Never in his life has he been so impatient for dawn to break, and the reason is that it's his first day of school. As twilight yields today, Clover feels time crawl like a lazy stream, stuck on the cusp between night and day. He has been awake since midnight, already bathed and dressed in his best clothes.

He looks at the well-worn watch on his wrist, its leather straps fraying but still functional. With a sigh, he checks the time again—perhaps the tenth time in as many minutes—but it doesn't make the hours go any faster. He still has two hours before he can relish dawn's first greetings.

Going back to bed is not an option. Sleep has vanished from his eyes, and the anticipation of the day ahead consumes him: the walk to school, finding his class, claiming a front-row seat, and absorbing all the lessons—each part of his mental forecast.

But first, he needs to relax. Since returning from the hospital, he has languished in his room, unwell and isolated. Forbidden from mingling or playing outside, he has dined alone, counting down the days until he can rejoin the world and step into the school he yearns to attend.

Starting Grade 1 is thrilling, especially since he skipped kindergarten entirely. With a smart brain—reading and writing since he was three—he has managed to advance a class. Yet, technically, he is still trailing by two years; he remains unshaken and confident in his ability to bridge the gap and reclaim lost ground. He has to.

None of the other children in the orphanage will be starting Grade 1 with him, as far as he knows. Most of his peers are advancing to Grade 3, leaving him the only one behind. He has often tried to confirm this with a few kids to ensure he wouldn't have anyone sitting with him in class, but he has been barred from speaking with anyone. His punishment still prevents him from participating in activities and preparing for the school year.

For the past three weeks, this has been his life. It hasn't changed much; in fact, he has managed to conserve his energy by avoiding conversations with people like Rodney and Rina.

Today, however, he is restless. The morning dallies in its emergence, so he considers going outside for a short stroll to calm his nerves, promising himself to return before anyone wakes up.

He quietly exits his room, carefully making his way down the stairs, his feet softly pressing against the creaking planks as if protesting his sneaky escape. He holds his breath, praying that no one hears him—especially Agatha.

Finally, he reaches the door. After unfastening the lock, he steps outside.

The world beyond still slumbers under a blanket of blue and purple, with stars gradually fading and hinting at the imminent arrival of dawn. He wraps his arms around himself, feeling the slight chill of the early morning air against his skin.

His footsteps echo on the empty streets, his nose already a hue of delicate pink, now transforming into a meandering brook due to the nipping air. Clover has never seen the city this quiet; the distant mountains are visible, appearing like a wet painting.

He is glad to take a morning walk but must stay close to home, no matter how enticing the world seems. A metal bench comes into view near a lamppost, wet with dewdrops, and he settles onto it, watching as the city gradually comes to life. The first signs of movement emerge in the windows of houses. The distant sound of a car engine starting up and the soft rustling of trees fill the air.

He wants to take it all in, but the time has come to return to his orphanage. The skies are lighter now, streaks of pink and orange heralding the arrival of Helios' chariot.

Turning back toward the orphanage, he carries with him a sense of peace—a calm that will help him face the day.

Clover returns to Whispering Hearts and goes straight to his room, sitting on his bed, which squeaks beneath him. He waits.

After a while, sunbeams peek into his room. The sun has risen, and now that it has, Clover gets ready for breakfast and heads downstairs into the hall.

He enters; it is deserted, but the matron is already there.

"Hello, Mrs. Wringer," he says, waving to the elderly woman behind the counter.

She wears a white dress and a scarf, her thin, wrinkled lips forming a smile. "Hello, dear Clover. Want some pancakes?"

Naturally, the answer is yes. *Who in their right mind would refuse pancakes?* Clover thinks, and his stomach rumbles in agreement, urging him to dash to the matron. "I'll take two with dark maple syrup."

He stretches his neck to peer over the counter, where the enticing aroma of warm pancakes wafts. A large bottle of dark syrup sits next to Mrs. Wringer.

"Of course," she says, ladling two pancakes onto a plate and drizzling them with syrup. Slicing a handful of bananas, she offers them to him with a smile. "Get more before everyone gets in here, all right?"

Clover takes the plate to his table and devours the pancakes. They are delicious—sweet and warm. He likes things warm. The banana, however, is unripe, its fibrous texture grating against his mouth. But he decides not to let a morsel go to waste. He finishes his plate and looks toward Mrs. Wringer, who smiles and gestures for him to get more.

Clover wonders why she is so kind to him. Maybe she notices him being bullied by Rodney and his clique. Despite Rodney being an orphan like him, his nature is cruel—very cruel.

Craving another serving of pancakes, he approaches Mrs. Wringer when suddenly a heavy boot stomps down on his foot. "Ouch!" he cries out, stumbling to the ground. The melamine plate flies from his hands, spinning in midair.

Rodney and his friends have arrived in the hall. "Where were you going, girly boy?" His clan—consisting of several boys and the only girl, Rina—laughs at Clover.

Clover remains on the ground, inhaling dust from the floor. The filth clings to his clothes, but it is trivial, for his prime wish remains to avoid the oppressive eclipse of disgrace, so nobody calls him a girly boy.

Taking a sharp breath, he gets to his feet, brushing the dirt off his navy sweater—a lotus flower crocheted on its front—his mind wandering through the labyrinth of unknown causes for bullying, bereft of the why and wherefore.

He slowly turns to Rodney, but he knows he is forbidden to speak, as the punishment remains in force. If he speaks, he breaks the rule and invites further repercussions from Agatha. Aware of Rodney's intention to goad him into speaking, he wisely refrains, sighs, picks up the plate from the floor, and heads toward Mrs. Wringer.

But he notices she isn't there anymore. "Where did she go?" he mutters.

With Mrs. Wringer absent from the hall, he now understands the source of Rodney's effrontery; he has perfectly seized the opportunity for mischief. But he goes one step further, grabbing Clover's already fragile sweater and tearing it apart.

Clover gasps, ensuring no words slip from his tongue; it is just a gasp —pure air, with no sound. But he knows what Rodney has done. His fingers tremble gingerly as they touch the torn fabric around his shoulders.

The sweater he has carefully preserved for the new school year is now torn apart. His excitement curdles into a bitter blend of anger and help-lessness. Pain pulses through him, and while his eyes cannot verify the magnitude of the tear, he sees the damage inflicted upon the garment as the white shirt beneath becomes visible.

Yet amidst the fury in his eyes, there is immense sadness. It is a senseless act of cruelty, something he endures regularly, but today he wasn't expecting any mishap.

Rodney proves himself once again, just being himself—cruel and pathetic.

Forbidden to retaliate or voice his anguish, his lips part as if to utter a flood of protests, yet the invisible chains of obedience stifle any audible outcry. Every fiber of his being screams in defiance, his eyes becoming an ocean of unspoken rage, longing for revenge.

"Oops! Sorry." Rodney throws his hand in the air while his friends laugh at Clover, who has become the subject of their derision.

The torn sweater he wears mirrors the torn symmetry of his existence.

Clover seethes with a desire for vindication, and in a brave moment, he lunges toward Rodney, his eyes widening, tears welling. With a valiant strike, he leaves his handprints on Rodney's cheeks.

The throng pauses; Rodney, befuddled and crimson-cheeked, stands silent.

Rina clings to his arm, her voice squeaky and irritating. "Are you okay, Rodney?"

Here stands Clover, unshaken, his eyes incandescent with anger, unwilling to budge an inch. Rodney blinks like an owl, and sensing his blunder—and perhaps fearing Clover—he flees, his companions in tow.

Clover watches them depart, proud of his act of bravery. But now what? His sweater is torn, his fingers brushing against the jagged edges of the rip. *Maybe it can be fixed.*

He retreats to his dormitory, yanks off his sweater, and examines the damage. The hole is quite large and cannot be concealed by a pin. He begins rummaging through his cupboard for a worthy piece of clothing for his first day of school. He checks the top shelf and the bottom; everything he owns has been worn multiple times.

He longs for something new, something special for his first day—something he can keep for memory's sake. But there is nothing.

Clover collapses to the floor, drained and overwhelmed. In a fit of frustration, he tosses the sweater aside, now beyond repair. Then, a glimmer of hope catches his eye: a jacket, crumpled and forgotten on the bottom shelf, obsidian in color. Curiously, he retrieves it, finding it nearly new, untouched by wear. He slips it on, and despite its slight largeness, he folds the cuffs to mitigate the size.

"This is good," he says, a smile returning to his face.

With his hands ensconced in his pockets and ready to depart, Clover chances upon something crumpled inside—initially deemed mere paper, but upon withdrawing it reveals itself to be paper bills: fives and tens. A treasure, he lays them out on the ground, counting with growing surprise —five, ten, twenty-five, forty-five—and halting at seventy-five. His face lights up at the unexpected money snuggled within the garment, a bounty never before witnessed by his eyes.

He ponders why fate has presented him with this exact amount, the selfsame tally as his debt to James for the ring. His heart fills with gratitude; he is thankful to Rodney for tearing his sweater, for without that, he would never have discovered this jacket, and the serendipitous riches would have remained hidden.

He shoves the money into his pocket, which for the first time ever bears a ponderous heft—a feeling that evokes happiness in Clover. At the same time, he is perplexed by the unexpected sum, wondering whether its previous owner, in a moment of oblivion, tucked the money inside and inadvertently bequeathed it to the orphanage—a situation he deems nothing short of a blessing.

Now, he heads out. It is time to repay James for his generosity. Swinging the bag onto his shoulder, he runs down the stairs and steps outside the orphanage.

The bag is light, containing only what Agatha gave him the night before—pencils, a notebook, and the bag itself, which he assumes once belonged to an older child from the residence. But he is happy. The bag remains in excellent shape, except for the zippers, which often jam. On the side, a netted pocket intended for a water bottle sits empty.

He longs for one, yet Agatha thinks it unnecessary. There will be plenty of water fountains at school, she has told him.

It is September 7, 1999. The air has warmed slightly, losing the cool, crisp quality of early dawn. Clover is a little too early for school, but he does not mind. Earlier is better; this way, he'll have plenty of time to find his class and maybe claim a seat in the front row.

On the cobbled road, he strides with an upbeat gait. Clover glances around, noticing the town awakening—shop shutters rising, morning strolls with furry companions, and balconies hosting sun-drenched moments for residents. Birdsong fills the morning air, and the distant mountains create a breathtaking sight.

From across the road, he looks at the artisan gallery, the moment ripe for returning the favor with the exact seventy-five dollars.

Clover crosses the road and stands before the gallery when James appears.

"Hello!" James greets him. "Good morning, Clover."

"Good morning, sir," Clover replies. "I'm glad you're here. I came to pay for the ring."

James furrows his brows, looking at him curiously. "Really?"

Clover hesitates, then pulls out the exact amount from his pocket and presents it to James with a flourish. "I just found the money in this jacket. I thought it was meant for you, so I came straight here."

James opens his mouth, skeptical of Clover's claim. "Exactly seventy-five?"

Clover nods. "Yes, sir."

James is slightly reluctant but accepts the money, placing it in his pocket. "It seems to me," he remarks, "that you have some blessing over your head."

Clover shrugs naively. "I don't know, sir. When I saw the money, I thought of you. So, I'm here to return your favor. The Lake Fairy liked the ring very much. Thank you. You are very kind, sir."

James, wreathed in a smile, looks at Clover, but his expression shifts to bemusement at the mention of the fairy. Shaking his head, he assumes Clover must have given the ring to a woman he calls Lake Fairy. His smile returns as he says, "First day of school, is it?"

Clover nods but says nothing.

"All right, then. Good luck!"

Clover bids him goodbye and retraces his familiar route to school, a path he has memorized through countless visits. He has walked this route frequently, yet never breached the school's territory, so today's walk feels like a rehearsed choreography.

He recalls halting outside the school gate during past walks, watching his peers' daily procession into the building. The walls, the gates, the classrooms—everything that was once a mystery to Clover—is now within his reach.

Everything changes today. Standing before the formidable gates, his heart flutters like a caged bird hungering for freedom. It's his moment—his day—when the boundary between spectator and participant dissolves. Clover nudges the gate but finds it firmly shut, perhaps too early for entry.

Left with no choice, he waits, fiddling with the iron bars as he peers inside like an eager inmate eyeing an escape. But for him, it's about entry, not escape.

A guard emerges next to Clover. "Whatchu doin' here, boy?" He wears a sky-blue uniform, with a badge displaying his name: Troy.

"Hello, sir," Clover says meekly. "I came early." He withdraws his hands from the gate.

"Too early, I tell ya," Troy says, yanking a massive bunch of keys from his pocket and opening the gate. "Come in, then."

Elation floods Clover as he's beckoned inside the school. He inhales deeply, stepping tentatively forward, goosebumps covering his body and a smile crossing his face.

As he passes through the main entrance, he finally discovers what a school looks like from the inside. The lobby sprawls grandly, with a desk at its center, temporarily vacant. Picture frames line the walls, their faces unknown to Clover yet evidently celebrated within the premises. Proud cabinets house shining trophies that tell tales of triumph. Green boards showcase an array of pinned photographs, paintings, and drawings.

Clover is thrilled. The guard is busy flicking on the lights. Clover approaches him and asks, "Where can I find the Grade 1 classroom?"

Troy seems uninterested in speaking with him; he ignores Clover and finishes lighting up the area.

"Sir?" Clover asks again.

Troy picks up the newspaper from the desk and settles into his chair. "Down the hall, third room to yer right."

"Thanks," Clover says, launching himself toward the direction Troy indicated.

He finds his classroom, which is deserted. Empty benches—no students yet. The walls are colorful, decorated with many posters: alphabets, numbers, shapes, fruits, and vegetables. Clover knows it all. He feels proud. *Maybe I can skip Grade 1, too.*

He settles into the first chair in the front row. The desk has storage space inside. "Wow!" He places his pencils and notebook there and patiently waits for the rest of the students to arrive.

As students begin to flock in, the room fills up. Clover eagerly scans the faces; some return his smile while others remain indifferent.

A boy sits next to him. Clover beams at him, and the boy reciprocates. He considers a handshake but pauses as the teacher arrives.

The clock strikes nine, and classes commence.

Seven

THE NEW FRIEND

"Good morning, everyone." A female teacher glides into the classroom, placing her satchel and a stack of books on the desk. "Welcome to Grade 1," she says. "My name is Regina Clarkson. You can call me Ms. Clarkson. All right?"

She brushes back her bobbed hair, straightens her glasses, pushes up her sleeve, and turns toward the board behind her, writing the date on it. Color seems never to have touched her frost-kissed pallor, her mulberry lips a vivid contrast to her complexion. Her spectacles are thick and oval, with green frames. Overall, she looks good—but different.

She retrieves a register from the desk and runs her fingers through it. "I'll be going around to everyone, tallying it against my list of students just to make sure we have everyone here. I should be familiar with your faces and names. So, starting from the last row, far left, please say your name..."

The roll call begins from the back row, with Meghan Brown's voice starting the process. Benjamin Martinez and a series of other names follow, the students responding in turn. Eva Thompson from the middle row, then Elijah Smith, and Chloe Williams join in, with introductions continuing.

Clover anticipates his turn, knowing he will be the last. After a string of around twenty names, the spotlight shifts to the student beside him. Ethan Verdi introduces himself with a smile.

Now it's Clover's moment. His heart quickens.

Ms. Clarkson adjusts her spectacles and looks at her register. "Clover, is it?"

"Clover Nelson," he adds, emphasizing the surname he holds dear.

"Okay, great." Ms. Clarkson places the register on the desk. "We have everyone now." She begins to roam among the students. "First, we'll do an activity to explore counting and grouping. You'll work together in pairs to create something interesting using those colorful blocks." She points to a bin of blocks at the room entrance.

"Amazing!" Clover exclaims, looking forward to finally getting his hands on the blocks.

The bin looks incredibly full, which he finds even more exciting. The boy next to him, Ethan, hears his excitement and smiles back.

"Your task is simple: work together to create something with these blocks. But remember, you must use exactly twenty blocks. Am I clear?" Ms. Clarkson says.

The students gather, discussing strategies and ideas. Clover looks at Ethan, and Ethan looks at Clover.

"Let's go," Ethan says.

Clover gets up from his seat, and they head to the bin housing the blocks together.

"Twenty for each group," Ms. Clarkson reminds everyone of the rules.

"Let's count them first," Emily says to her partner, Chloe. "Then we can plan what to build."

Meanwhile, Ethan moves through the crowd, grabs a handful of blocks, spreads them on the ground, and looks to Clover. "Can you help me count?"

"Of course." Clover sits down.

They count exactly twenty and carry them back to their seats.

"Why don't we make a tower?" Ethan suggests. "It'll be the easiest and fastest."

"Yes, but that's way too easy." Clover taps his chin. "Why don't we make a car?"

Ethan nods. "Okay. A car."

Other groups also launch into fervent discussions, their schemes gradually taking shape. Some number the blocks, while others conjure imaginative skyscrapers, towers, figures, and other forms. All students deploy their arithmetic skills.

Ms. Clarkson roams between each group, observing and encouraging the students. The classroom has transformed into a workshop of creativity, where students explore the concepts of grouping and counting in a hands-on, interactive manner.

Clover enjoys it, too. Even though he is the oldest in the class and knows more than his classmates, he doesn't overtly display it. The room hums with laughter, shared discoveries, and the sounds of blocks clinking together.

After about thirty minutes, Ms. Clarkson addresses her students again. "Is everyone done?"

Ethan and Clover have finished. Instead of a car, what they've created looks more like a truck. They don't know what it is, but they proudly sit beside their creation.

Ms. Clarkson surveys each project, applauding and commending the students. Her gaze falls upon Ethan and Clover. "A truck. Very well done."

This little admiration sends a flurry of butterflies through Clover's stomach. Never before has he been appreciated. His face glows with newfound confidence. He turns to Ethan. "See? She liked it."

Ethan nods, but not very enthusiastically.

"Now I'll be reading a story to you," Ms. Clarkson says. Every ear is tuned to her with absolute focus. "The story is called *The Sea Turtle and the Little Starfish*." She begins to narrate:

"Once upon a time, in the vast, sparkling sea, there lived a turtle named Orlea. Orlea was the slowest in the whole sea, with a dull, mottled shell and droopy eyes. All other sea creatures, including his own kin, made fun of him. But he was kind and wise, always ready to help those in need.

"One stormy night, Orlea found a little starfish far from home, crying softly inside a coral reef. *What's wrong?* Orlea asked.

I'm lost, the starfish replied, whose name was Terra. *I can't find my way back to Starfish Cove.*

"Orlea understood the ocean could be a scary place for a little starfish.

He was wise, and his shell was sturdy. *I'll help you,* Orlea said. *You can sit on my back, and I'll take you to your cove.*

"Terra rested upon Orlea's shell, and together they set off on their journey, talking and laughing, sharing stories and adventures. Terra realized how kind Orlea was.

"After a long swim, they finally reached Starfish Cove. Terra's family was overjoyed to see her and thanked Orlea for his kindness. *You're a hero,* Terra said to Orlea.

"Word of Orlea's bravery spread throughout the sea, and soon every creature knew of the humble turtle who had saved the young starfish. From that day on, Orlea was no longer just an 'ugly' turtle. He was respected and loved by all."

The tale draws its final breath with Ms. Clarkson shutting the book and prompting, "So, who can tell me the moral of this story?"

A few hands shoot up in the air. Ms. Clarkson points to a girl in the back. "Miranda, is that right?"

"Yes," says a girl with brunette hair and buck teeth.

"All right, Miranda. What do you think the moral is?"

Miranda scans the room nervously, then says, "That we should help others in need."

Ms. Clarkson nods. "Good. Anyone else?"

Clover raises his hand.

"Oh, Clover," Ms. Clarkson points to him, "go ahead."

Clover sweeps his gaze around, finding himself the center of attention. He clears his throat and says, "The story's moral is that kindness is above external beauty. Regardless of how you look, the goodness of the heart truly matters."

"Very good, Clover." Ms. Clarkson gives a subdued clap. "The true value lies in kindness, so be kind to everyone."

Proud of his answer, Clover looks at Ms. Clarkson, expecting her to delve deeper into the story's moral essence, seeking a richer harvest of appreciation for his excellent response. But he soon realizes her delivery is too mechanical, as if she has repeated the words countless times before and the story's original enthusiasm has long since faded.

Throughout her narration, no smile sported her face, and she appeared inherently disinterested. He wonders if she practices what she teaches or if her job is just a job devoid of passion. Nevertheless, Clover finds himself enjoying the class and looks at Ethan, who appears enervated, his eyes shutting down in boredom. Clover nudges him from his seat, and Ethan awakens with a start.

"Is there a problem, Ethan?" Ms. Clarkson notices Ethan dozing off and Clover trying to wake him.

"No—nothing, Ms. Clarkson." Ethan straightens his back.

"Hmm." Ms. Clarkson furrows her brows. She turns to the class. "Next, we'll do numbers. Everyone, open your math textbook."

While everyone else opens their textbooks, Clover has none. Ethan has one, too. Clover peers at Ethan's book and notices the printed numbers along with colorful pictures.

"Don't you have your own book?" Ethan asks, noticing Clover looking at his.

"No," Clover replies. "I did… not know."

Ethan finds it odd. "It was on the list. Didn't your parents read it?"

Clover feels a sinking sensation in his stomach. He goes quiet, bowing his head and twiddling his fingers.

Ms. Clarkson notices Clover without the book. "May I ask why you don't have your book open yet?"

Clover looks up. His stomach aches. "Umm…" His voice feels trapped, unsure of what's happening. There is a sudden pain in his stomach, a strange and unwonted sensation, as if his intestines want to release the detritus within. He kneads his stomach, still without an answer.

"Do you understand me?" Ms. Clarkson asks again, her voice bearing a conspicuous austerity.

Clover needs to go; nature calls. "May I please go to the restroom?" Although he emptied the morning's depths, he feels the need to go again.

Ms. Clarkson's lips form a tight line, her stare disdainful. "The lesson has just started."

"Please, Ms. Clarkson," Clover begs, kneading his abdomen. "Let me go."

Ethan starts to worry. "Miss, it looks like, um… Clover has a tummy ache. Please let him go."

Flashing a look of scorn, Ms. Clarkson says, "Fine. You may go."

Once outside the classroom, Clover breaks into a run, not stopping or looking back. He has no idea where the restroom is, wandering like a solitary cloud in a barren sky.

Troy strolls into the corridor and spots Clover's face turning red and contorting as if he is having a fit. "What's up, boy?" he asks.

"Restroom!" Clover squeezes his glutes, one hand on his stomach, the other pinching his pants.

Troy looks at him condescendingly. "Don't ya know how ter read?" He points to the sign affixed to the wall in front of them. "Boys, the last one on yer left."

"Thanks!" Clover runs in that direction.

He pushes open the last door—the beige one—and is greeted by the stench of bleach. Without wasting any time, he heads to the first stall. The breath he has been holding is released; his gut relaxes, and he feels relieved.

As he comes out to wash his hands, he notices a few basins against the wall: curved, yellowed, and slightly larger than the sinks. Beads of sweat form on his forehead as he steps closer, surprised and wondering about their purpose. There is no one inside. Who might he ask?

Retreating to the sink, he turns on the faucet, his mind still consumed by the unusual basins. The water is cool; he splashes his face, wipes it with a paper towel, and exits.

Once again, he stands in the corridor, reluctant to return to class. He doesn't have a math textbook because he doesn't have parents, unaware that there was a supply list. Angry at Agatha for not ensuring he had the necessary materials, he feels woeful, worrying he will become a joke once again.

Tears spill from his eyes. He weeps as he sinks to the ground, leaning against the wall. His maiden day at school, purportedly meant to be good and full of nice things and fun activities, turns out to be a disaster. Ms. Clarkson, erstwhile amiable, later reveals a strict demeanor. Clover wonders why she had looked at him with disgust. He simply forgot his textbook, yet shame overwhelms him.

The mortification deepens as nature calls, disrupting the lesson. His stomach churns, replaying the incident in his mind. He has become a laughingstock once again. *What happened?* He doesn't know the answer but attributes it to his anxiety.

Time passes, and the bell rings. Clover stands up. *Why did the bell ring?* Does that mean they get to go home?

Clover doesn't realize it's lunchtime. He stares at his classroom, waiting for the students to come out. But it's Ms. Clarkson who emerges, striding toward him. His stomach plummets again.

"Clover!" she yells. "Where have you been?"

"I... was... in the..." Clover gulps and opens his mouth but fails to form a coherent sentence.

"In my office right now," she commands, flitting past him.

Acquiescing, Clover follows her.

Ms. Clarkson leads him to her office, which isn't far away. Soon, they are inside a large room with multiple cubicles. Ms. Clarkson enters her cubicle and sits down with a thud. "Sit," she instructs.

Clover complies.

"Where were you?" she asks, removing her spectacles.

"In the restroom, miss."

Ms. Clarkson steeples her hands, a curious look on her face. "And... which one did you go to?"

"Er..." Clover is puzzled by the question. "The one on the... um... the last one."

"Left or right?"

Clover is confused. "Left, I think."

Ms. Clarkson rolls her eyes. "You'll go to General. Do you understand?"

Clover furrows his brows. "What is General?"

Ms. Clarkson heaves a sigh. "For general staff, not for students. It's right next to this staff room. The sign says: *Staff Only.* Do you understand?"

Clover scratches his chin, pondering. "But why?"

Ms. Clarkson puts her spectacles back on, resting them on her crooked nose. "It's because you're special. So even if your friends insist, you'll only use our staff restroom. Is that clear?"

Pride surges within Clover, a newfound privilege granting him access to the sanctum of staff. His chest swells. "Am I really that special?"

Ms. Clarkson shakes her head, her gaze fixed on her register. "Go back, Clover. It's lunchtime."

It's the middle of the break—lunchtime and playtime for students. Clover exits the staff room and finds the corridor almost empty, wondering where everyone is. *They must be outside,* he thinks.

His footsteps lead him to his classroom, which is nearly deserted. He finds only Ethan, who jumps up at the sight of him.

"Where were you, Clover? Are you okay? Do you need a doctor?"

Clover looks at him with deep appreciation, relieved to find someone waiting for him. "I'm okay," he says. "Just some—uh—stomach pain."

"Oh!" Ethan sits back down, pressing his hand to his chest. "Are you sure you don't want any medicine?"

Clover settles into his chair. "No, I think I'm good."

"All right, then." Ethan opens his bag, which appears to be brand new, with perfectly functioning zippers and the faint smell of fresh fabric. "Let's eat before the bell rings again." He takes out a red lunchbox with a spoon and fork affixed to its lid. With a click, he opens it to reveal a whitish-looking dish inside—perhaps potato salad—along with some strawberries, crackers, and toast.

"Wow!" Clover's mouth drops open, his gaze fixed on the meal.

"Come on," Ethan says. "Open yours."

Clover averts his eyes, realizing it's rude because his mouth is watering.

Ethan tilts his head. "Don't you want to eat?"

Time stands still. Clover lacks the courage to confess that he doesn't have lunch, oblivious to the fact that this is a common norm. He assumed the school kitchen would provide meals like his orphanage's kitchen.

"I—I don't have lunch," Clover says hesitantly, his head lowered.

"What?" Ethan asks, a perplexed expression on his face. "How can your parents send you without lunch?"

Clover is silent. It's painful to hear this repeatedly. *Your parents this, your parents that...* He is tired of it.

"Oh!" Ethan says, smacking his forehead. "They must have given you lunch money. Right?"

Clover slumps quietly, his shoulders drooping under the weight of his empty stomach and heavy heart. He rests his head on the table, nearly on the verge of tears. He has no lunch, nor do his pockets jingle with lunch money. It's sad. He thought Agatha had equipped him with everything he needed for school, but that wasn't the case, and perhaps it never would be.

First, he suffers the torment of having no textbook, and now he feels the shame of lacking a lunch. A deep sadness settles in his heart, and in the stillness of his pain, he stifles his sobs, whimpering in silence.

Ethan closes his lunchbox, leans closer to Clover, and places his hand on his shoulder. "Your parents didn't give you any, right?" His voice is filled with sympathy, but Clover doesn't want it. He fears confiding in Ethan about his parents will elicit pity, resulting in daily reminders of his situation. He wishes to avoid that altogether. He wants to be normal, just like him.

Clover lifts his head and looks at Ethan. "It's just that... they forgot. I was in a hurry." His cheeks flush pink at the lie that spills from his mouth.

"That's okay," Ethan reassures him. "You can have mine, and we'll share it. Here." He places his lunchbox on Clover's table, nudging him to eat from it.

Clover's stomach growls, empty and aching. "Okay," he says quietly.

Ethan peers at Clover with fondness, pleased to share his meal. This small act of kindness bridges the gap between two once-strangers. As they sit together, exchanging bites and stories, a bond begins to form. Clover has finally found a dawn in his night, a friend dispelling the darkness in his life.

Eight

THE ADVENTURES OF SCHOOLYARD COMPANIONS

The bell rings, and the classes conclude. The first day of school is over. Clover and Ethan, two newfound best friends, exit the school grounds, laughing, chatting, and enjoying each other's company.

A lavish car is parked at the entrance, with the driver standing outside, waving to Ethan.

"Is that your car?" Clover asks Ethan.

Ethan nods. "Yes, that's Mr. Manson over there. He's our driver."

"I see," Clover says, edging closer to the car.

The door swings open, and he steals a glance inside, mesmerized by what he sees: tan leather seats and a subtle fragrance of pine. Every detail is immaculate—just perfect. This car holds no disorder, unlike Agatha's perpetually cluttered vehicle, filled with scattered coffee cups and stray napkins. Her car often has an assortment of items littered throughout, with bottles occasionally rolling out from their hiding spots beneath the seats. But this vehicle is spotless, as if brand new.

"Okay, Clover. I'll see you tomorrow," Ethan says as he sits inside the car. The driver closes the door, bringing Clover back to reality. The window winds down as he steps back, and Ethan leans out. "Bye, Clover."

Clover waves. "Bye." A soft murmur escapes as he watches Ethan being chauffeured away in a richly tended vehicle, while he must walk. Though his destination isn't far, the journey would surely be less tedious if his own ride were there to bear him afar. He shakes his head, realizing he is asking too much of his circumstances. He has just started school and is already wishing for a car. It feels like a far-fetched dream.

With a heavy sigh, he begins the homeward trek toward the orphanage. As he passes by the peppy hub of shops, Clover muses about Ethan's life. The type of vehicle that whisked Ethan away makes him wonder about the size of his house. He reaches the orphanage and climbs the stairs to the entryway. Would Ethan's house be bigger than this entire orphanage?

His dwelling—never quite feeling like home—stands still, guarding within its walls its identity as an orphanage, with no sign revealing its purpose. For this veil of anonymity, Clover is beyond grateful.

In the following days, Clover finds himself drawn to the school atmosphere. He is the first to arrive and the last to leave, all because of Ethan. The boy is a remarkable blend of generosity, empathy, and innate friendliness that sets him apart from the other students in their class. Ethan wears humility like a cloak, despite his wealth—a rare trait, according to Clover.

However, a recurring dilemma persists during lunch hours, and Clover does not know how to handle it. Unlike Ethan, he doesn't bring lunch to school and always makes excuses about his parents being out of town, late, or sometimes lazy. Without a lunchbox, he faces the challenge of empty hands during this midday ritual.

But Ethan is generous. After a few times, he stops asking Clover why he doesn't bring lunch and invariably offers him a portion of his meal. However, this makes Clover uncomfortable and embarrassed—a reminder of the disparity between the luxury of Ethan's world and Clover's reality of helplessness and hunger.

Despite his initial hesitance, Clover's attempts to evade the situation prove futile. Sneaking away during lunch only leads to the disheartening realization that Ethan has patiently waited for him all along. So, he gives in and happily shares Ethan's lunch every day.

It's a sunny Friday afternoon, and as usual, Ethan's car is waiting for him outside the school, right on time. Clover is ready to say goodbye as they prepare to depart for the weekend, but Ethan has a different idea.

"Why don't we go explore the city?" he suggests.

"You and me?" Clover asks, surprised.

"Of course! Who else would I be talking to?" Ethan chuckles.

Clover feels a surge of excitement but glances at Mr. Manson, who is leaning against the car with his arms crossed, looking around humdrumly.

"What about Mr. Manson?" Clover asks.

Ethan purses his lips. "I forgot about him." He walks toward Mr. Manson. Clover watches the two talk. Ethan seems persistent, but Mr. Manson shakes his head vigorously. Of course, it's a no. Who would let a child from such a family roam the city alone? Ethan returns to Clover, his head hanging low. "He said no."

"I knew it," Clover says, slumping his shoulders.

"How do you get to go around the city on your own?" Ethan asks.

Clover notices one of the straps on his bag coming loose. Really? He looks back at Ethan. "That's because I don't have..." He stops, realizing he was about to reveal too much. Sighing, he employs the other strap to hoist the bag onto his shoulder. "Um, it's because my parents aren't very strict."

"That's nice," Ethan says, pouting. "I wish I had your parents."

Clover nearly jumps. "No! Don't ever wish to have my parents."

Ethan raises his eyebrows. "Why not?"

"They are," Clover averts his eyes, "they are... not very caring, you know? Yours are better—and rich too."

Ethan rolls his eyes. "Oh, please. You should meet my mom. She's always doing something strange."

Clover narrows his eyes. "What's wrong with her?"

Ethan shrugs. "I don't know. Dad is great, though. He never lets Mom say anything to me, calls me a prince, and says I'm the son he always wanted—his heir." His cheeks flush with pride.

"Do you know what that means?" Clover folds his arms, a quiet smile on his lips.

"Do you?" Ethan asks.

"I do, yes."

"Hmm, I know too. It means..." Ethan's speech halts. "Er, I think I know what it is," he says, scratching his head, as if the words, like shy shadows, slip from his reach. "Actually, I forgot."

Clover finds Ethan's innocent antics amusing. "You don't know what it means, Ethan. Just admit it," he says. "Did you ever ask him in the first place?"

Ethan shakes his head. "Yeah, I never did."

"Ask your dad next time," Clover suggests, glancing over at Mr. Manson. "Now how do we convince him?"

"Hmm." Ethan taps his finger to his lips, and suddenly, a thought strikes him. "Let me go talk to him again."

This time, Ethan approaches Mr. Manson and returns quickly, a smile on his face. "He's agreed. Let's go!"

Clover wonders what Ethan said to convince Mr. Manson so quickly. "How did you manage that?"

Ethan purses his lips. "I told him I was going to your place and asked him to wait for me."

A lump forms in Clover's throat. "Are you really... coming to my place?"

"Not today. We won't have much time." Ethan grabs Clover's arm. "Come on, show me around."

Clover breathes a sigh of relief, and together they set off on their adventure.

"Where do you suggest we go first?" Ethan looks around in sheer awe, taking in the shops that unfold before him—a mélange of colorful sights, sounds, and aromas. The market stretches out, from stalls bursting with fresh fruits and vegetables to those lined with everyday groceries, from boutiques showcasing the latest trends to museums flooded with vestiges of yore. Ethan does not know where to start.

Clover, however, dives into intense cogitation. *Where should I take him? He'll insist on visiting my house if I don't pick a good place. What to do?*

"Tell me!" Ethan exclaims, his mouth and eyes wide with excitement.

An idea strikes Clover. "Giggling Sweets."

"A sweet shop?" Ethan asks.

"Yes," Clover says, leading him to the pedestrian crossing. "It's on the other side of the road."

They wait at the signal, too excited to run across just yet. The thrill of the afternoon rush fills them with pure joy. Finally, the pedestrian signal lights up, and the boys dash across.

Ethan vaults up and down. "Let's go, let's go!"

Clover shifts his bag to the other shoulder, snickering at Ethan's excitement. "Okay!"

The clouds begin to cover the sun. Ethan looks up. "I hope it doesn't rain. I don't have an umbrella."

"Don't know..." Clover mutters.

Suddenly, a whimsical candy shop springs into sight. Ethan spots it first. "Woah!"

"There it is," Clover says, guiding Ethan to the shop's window. "They have lots of treats inside, in different colors and shapes."

Ethan presses his face against the glass, his heart racing with anticipation. "What are we waiting for?"

Clover curls his lips, thinking, *I won't be buying anything. I don't have any money.* He steals a glance at Ethan's gleeful face. *Maybe I'll let Ethan go inside on his own and buy what he wants.*

"Clover, let's go!" Ethan bounds merrily.

Clover fidgets with his pocket, feeling the lone two-dollar coin inside. "I'll wait here for you," he says. "You go in and get what you want."

Ethan looks at him. "You're coming with me. Why do you want to wait here?"

"Er..." Clover looks away, swallowing hard. "I've been here many times, and it's boring to me now."

"Oh, come on." Ethan grabs Clover's arms. "One more time won't hurt. Let's go!"

They step into the shop, entering a world filled with vibrant colors and sugary delights. Shelves are lined with jars of colorful candies, and the air is heavy with the scents of confections, chocolates, and caramel.

As they explore further, the scent shifts, guiding them to a corner where they can smell licorice mingling with the invigorating freshness of peppermint and the pure sweetness of sugar. Their eyes wander from jar to jar, mesmerized by the various colors and flavors, eager to taste it all.

Other children flit around the shop like butterflies, urging their parents to fill their bags with treats. Parents look exhausted and concerned, yet unable to resist their children's wishes. Clover overhears a mother telling her daughter, "If you eat more than one a day, all your teeth will fall out, and you'll look like your grandma." The girl bursts into tears.

Clover moves ahead, wondering if Ethan will buy any sweets at all. "Are you going to get anything?" he asks.

Ethan's mouth hangs open as he takes in his surroundings, as if he's landed on another planet. "Umm-hmm."

"Er... then maybe get a basket?" Clover suggests, walking toward the front to grab one.

"Oh, yes." Ethan takes the basket from Clover. "I'll hold it."

From the first wall to the first shelf, he adds every variant of confectionery and sweet to his basket. Starting with a white-and-red candy cane, the assortment quickly expands to chocolates, licorice twists, sugared almonds, jawbreakers, gummy bears, and a plethora of other delectable treats.

Clover watches the sweets pile up in Ethan's basket and asks, "Will you really get all these?"

Ethan is still busy browsing. "I think so—maybe some more. I bet Mom won't approve, but I won't tell her."

"Do you have enough money for it?" Clover asks, genuinely curious but realizing he's asking the wrong person. Ethan comes from wealth, so why would affordability even be a question?

"I don't know; we'll see." Ethan shrugs nonchalantly.

"What do you mean, you don't know?" Clover asks, confused. "You should know how much money you're carrying."

Ethan places the basket on the counter. "I'm not carrying any money. I have my father's card. It just needs to be swiped."

Clover has never heard of that before. *Payment with a card?* he thinks.

Ethan pulls out a blue-grey card from his pocket and hands it to the cashier.

"Yes," Ethan replies. "Could you please swipe the card and process the payment?"

The confidence with which Ethan speaks to the cashier is something Clover can only dream of. Clearly, he's done this many times before. The cashier, however, seems hesitant and calls over her manager. The shop manager, wearing a red apron and a hat resembling a candy cane, approaches.

"What's going on?" Ethan asks, crossing his arms, unimpressed by the manager's arrival.

The manager, named Drew, leans over the counter. "Can you give me your father's phone number?"

Ethan shakes his head and pulls a business card from his other pocket. "I forgot to give you this."

The manager examines the card and exchanges glances with the cashier. "Very well, then," he says. "Go ahead, Amanda."

Drew walks away. The cashier looks at Ethan and Clover but proceeds to follow the manager's instructions. She swipes the card, and a receipt prints out.

"All set," she says. "I need a signature, please." She hands a pen to Ethan, who signs without hesitation. The cashier packs the treats into a bag and hands it to Ethan.

"Thank you," Ethan says, accepting the bag filled with plentiful treats.

As they exit the shop, Clover is curious. "How much was it all? And what did you give to the cashier?"

"It was a credit card—my dad's." Ethan takes a peek inside his bag. "And that's a lot of candy."

"It is," Clover says half-heartedly. "So, tell me, what is a credit card? Don't you need real money to make a payment?"

Ethan looks at Clover, surprised by his questions, which he thinks should be common knowledge. "You don't know what a credit card is? Don't your parents have one?"

Clover shakes his head. He would know if he had parents.

"Oh! Umm, I don't know exactly how it works, but it's my dad's. He says I have plenty of money to buy anything with his card." He shows the card off to Clover with flair.

"But the second card you gave," Clover asks, "what was that for?"

"That one," Ethan says, rummaging through his pockets, "is my dad's business card. On the back, he's written that I can use this card at will. He also put a dollar amount here... five-zero-zero."

Clover is alien to this concept but is surely drawn in. "That's cool—very cool, actually."

Ethan grins.

"How much were the candies?" Clover asks.

"I don't know," Ethan says. "Let's see, but it must be under five-zero-zero." He pulls the receipt from his bag. "Four-seven, dot, two-five."

Clover instinctively cups his cheeks with his hands. "That's a lot of money for candy."

"Yeah, I know." Ethan scans around for their next adventure. "Where should we go now?"

While Clover is genuinely happy for Ethan's carefree attitude toward money, he also feels a pang of jealousy at his friend's unrestrained spending. He realizes that this is something he will never be able to emulate.

"You froze again." Ethan gives him a gentle shake. "Let's cross the road."

After their olfactory adventures, the duo continues to explore, hopping from one shop to another. Ethan leads Clover into a toy store and buys a plush teddy bear for Clover and a train for himself.

"Thank you, Ethan." Clover's cheeks turn red. "But I didn't need it."

"No one needs toys," Ethan says, winking. "But aren't they nice to have?"

As the day progresses, the rumbles of hunger grow louder. With empty stomachs, the pair contemplates their next move.

"I am so hungry right now." Ethan sits on a bench outside the toy shop, Clover beside him. "Where should we go?"

Clover shrugs. He's never eaten out before. What counsel might he offer? Picking up their bags again, they stroll down the street, searching for a place to eat.

"I want something warm," Ethan says.

"Me too." Clover kneads his stomach. "I would love some cup noodles —warm and soupy. Yum!"

Ethan stops in his tracks and looks horrified at Clover. "Cup noodles?"

"Yeah, why?" Clover asks, but he soon realizes from Ethan's reaction that the disparity between rich and poor extends to food.

"That's dis—er, never mind." Ethan shakes his head. "You know," he turns to Clover with pity in his eyes, "your parents don't really seem to take good care of you."

Clover lowers his head, embarrassed, his lips parting but unable to form a logical response.

"Look at how skinny you are." Ethan pats his shoulder. "Do they give you cup noodles every day?"

Clover eats them every other day. That's the most common item donated to orphanages, so he's bound to have them often. "Yes," he says, still keeping his head down.

Ethan takes a deep breath. "Don't worry. We'll have proper food today, okay?"

Clover looks at him. *Proper food?* he muses, nodding but unsure what Ethan means by "proper food."

An eatery comes into view on their left. Halting in their tracks, they are drawn in by the mouthwatering aroma of savory dishes wafting through the air. They enter the eatery, where a pleasant-looking man greets them. Before they are seated, Ethan hands over the card he gave to the cashier earlier at the sweet shop.

The server nods and brings menus for both of them. Clover feels very nervous. A quick glance at his shoes and ordinary clothes drains his confidence and tells him he doesn't belong here. His pockets are empty, and he can't even afford water, but he remains seated because of his friend, who can only find his "proper food" here.

The place has rustic décor and a homely charm, but that does little to put Clover at ease. A wrinkle-free checkered cloth mantles the table, a clear film upon it. The server arrives with the menus, and Ethan promptly begins to skim through them. Clover doesn't pick up the menu, let alone decide what to eat.

"What do you want to eat?" Ethan asks, his eyes on the menu.

Clover wrings his hands and takes deep breaths. "Whatever you like."

Ethan smiles and whispers to him, "I think I'll order number four."

Clover looks at him. "What does it have?"

"I've had this dish before. Watch me." Ethan calls to the server with a wave of his palm.

The server approaches. "What would you like, sir?"

Ethan closes the menu and sets it aside. "Number four, please," he says with an aristocratic comportment. "For both of us."

"O-o-h. Fantastic choice." The server flashes a crooked smile, keeping his notepad tucked in his pocket. "Risotto with wild mushrooms. I'll bring it right up for you."

The server collects the menus and leaves.

"Risotto?" Clover asks. "And wild mushrooms? Wouldn't that make us sick?"

Ethan chuckles. "No, it won't. Don't worry."

Their meals arrive shortly after. Their conversation flows effortlessly between mouthfuls, mingling with the clinking of dishes as Ethan explains the types of meals he's used to at home, while Clover listens in amazement, having nothing fancy to share.

The boys revel in the joy of satisfying their hunger, their plates now empty save for remnants. They feel full. Clover has never had a meal like this before. When the bill arrives, Ethan, as usual, whips out his father's credit card, which magically pays for their meals.

As they exit, Ethan realizes it's too late. The sun has almost evanesced below the horizon, and the chill in the air is increasing. "Oh no. We must go back," he tells Clover.

They hurry across the street toward the school, weaving through the crowd, gliding over the cobbled path, rushing past the shops until they spot Ethan's car parked outside the school, just where it was.

Clover and Ethan are both out of breath.

Mr. Manson emerges from the vehicle, looking relieved. "Oh, thank goodness," he says, claiming Ethan's schoolbag. "I was getting worried, sir. Where have you been?"

"Sorry, Mr. Manson," Ethan says, drawing a sharp breath. "We got busy playing." He flickers an eyelid at Clover, who stands nearby, clutching his own bag with his teddy bear inside.

Mr. Manson eyes the bags the boys hold but refrains from asking anything. "All right, sir. Please get in. We're late." He opens the passenger door for him.

Ethan quickly removes a handful of treats from his bag and shoves them into Clover's.

"Please, I don't want them," Clover protests.

"No. How can I eat so much alone?"

Clover peers into his bag, his teddy bear now surrounded by the sugary treasures Ethan has shared. A faint smile spreads across his lips. With Ethan comfortably seated in the car, the moment of parting draws imminent, making Clover acutely aware of his impending return to the orphanage. He watches Ethan drive away before slowly turning toward his own destination, Whispering Hearts.

Nine

❧

THE BULLY'S REQUITAL

Clover enters his orphanage, wishing he had more time with Ethan and could even go to his place, but that seems absurd. *Why would Ethan invite me to his house?* Even if he did, Clover would have to reciprocate, and he has been lying about his parents the entire time. It could damage their friendship. It has been a long time since he found a friend.

Lost in thought, he goes upstairs, the bag containing the teddy bear and treats in his hands. He opens his dorm room and finds someone sitting on his bed—two people, in fact.

"Hello, girly boy." Rodney is lounging on Clover's bed, claiming it as his own. "What took you so long?"

Clover remembers his encounter with Rodney earlier in the week, the smack to his face delivered by his own hand. He doesn't go to the same school as Rodney. He's older, likely in middle school, but Clover isn't sure. Since the incident on Monday, Rodney and his friends have been absent, which made Clover's life a bit easier. He thought he had managed to repel them for good, but he was wrong. Rodney's body language clearly indicates he is here to settle the score.

"May I ask what you're doing in my room?" Clover thinks that if he speaks confidently, he might deter Rodney's decision.

"Ha!" Rodney smirks, approaching slowly with his hands shoved in his pockets, chewing on something—or perhaps just pretending to be cool. Clover swallows and instinctively hides the bag with his goodies behind him. Rodney angles his head, noticing the conspicuously large bag concealed behind Clover's small frame. "What's in there?"

Clover squeezes the handle. "Nothing," he says. "Just some stuff I got."

Rodney smirks again.

Clover wants to punch him in the face.

"From where?" Rodney flutters his barely-there eyelashes.

Clover clenches his teeth. "That's none of your business."

"It is, girly boy." Rodney ambles around the room, stretching his neck every so often.

Cringe, Clover thinks. "Can you stop that?" He parts his lips, disgust evident on his face. "Doing that neck thing?"

Rodney stops, raises his brows, and leans toward him. "I think you've forgotten your place."

Rina stands behind Rodney, a bully in female form, equally ruthless and demanding. "Show him his place, Rodney. I'll lock the door."

Rodney rolls up his sleeve, catching Clover's eye while he thinks about the day's unexpected fortunes. What a good day it was, filled with shopping adventures, good food, and the company of his new friend. Yet, in an ill-timed twist of fate, he finds himself under the same roof as Rodney, who is now approaching him with a sinister smile, his yellowed teeth making him appear even more menacing. His demeanor suggests he might excel as a future candidate for gangsterism or thievery. His blue eyes delve into Clover's sable pools. "You'll regret what you did that day."

In his discomposure, Clover lets slip the bag, prompting Rina to swiftly snatch it and peer inside.

"A teddy bear!" Rina pulls the giant stuffed toy from the bag. "It's huge. Look, Rodney."

"It's mine. Don't touch it," Clover blurts out, his ears turning scarlet.

Rodney tilts his head. "Strange that you call this teddy bear yours. It's not. You must have stolen it."

"I did not." Clover gulps, his throat dry. "My f—friend bought it for me."

"Your friend?" Rina grimaces, shoving her hair behind her ears. "How come you have a friend?"

Rina's facial expressions hurt Clover more than her voice. "Can you not shut up?" he snaps, shaking his head.

Rina parts her lips, digging her nails into the plush teddy bear. "How dare you?" She looks at Rodney. "Did you hear him? He told me to shut up." She then snuggles the bear, pouting her lips and trying to look cute—but bullies can never look good to Clover.

Rodney snorts like a bull ready to charge. "Enough, girly boy." His face twitches as he pins Clover to the wall. "Your hands were flying that day. You smacked me in front of my friends. Where did you get the confidence from?"

Clover feels Rodney's garlic breath on his face, so he holds his breath and restrains himself from speaking. *I don't know,* he thinks.

Rodney recoils, taking a sharp breath, and staggers backward. His muscles tense, and Clover can tell he is seething with anger, his eyes blinded by hate. He rolls his shoulders like springs beneath the fabric of his sleeves, his hands curling into tight fists, arms trembling intensely. Now, Clover is afraid, and he knows what's coming.

Rina smirks behind Rodney, watching the impending confrontation with excitement. The only thing missing is the popcorn. Rodney lunges toward Clover, and with a guttural growl, he unleashes his rage—his fist aimed at Clover's face—and time seems to slow down. Rodney's knuckles collide with Clover's cheek, a collision of flesh against flesh, one's knobby crests pressing into the hollows of the other's. Clover cannot see anything; shockwaves shoot up his arm, making him numb—numb to pain, numb to reaction. He drops to the floor, breathing heavily, overwhelmed with searing humiliation, momentarily disconnecting from the tangible world.

"How did that feel?" Rodney blows on his fist, evaluating it with a pugilist's flair. "Want some more?"

Rina jumps excitedly. Clover watches her celebrate from the corner of his barely open eyes. However, her face is blurred, and he is more than grateful for that.

The symphony of the previous strike fades. Rodney hauls for another blow, his breaths ragged, his knuckles still stinging, and this time the target is Clover's stomach. With his foot, he pounds into Clover's midriff.

Clover winces, tears welling, while Rodney laughs triumphantly. Rina claps, thrilled by Rodney's performance, elated at Clover's plight. Revenge has been exacted, and it cost Clover dearly. He hit Rodney once, and in return, he received two strikes.

Rodney lowers his head and looks Clover in the eye. "I'm not done yet. You hit me in front of everyone. Rina!" he calls. "Bring everyone in here."

Rina places the teddy bear on the bed, unlatches the door, and leaves the room. Supine on the floor, Clover braces himself for a wider audience to witness his humiliation.

As footsteps fill the room, he remains still while Rodney, at the center, addresses his group. "Watch, everyone. This is what happens when you mess with Rodney."

Rina snickers and claps enthusiastically.

"Look at him on the floor, crying in pain. Yet this girly boy dared to hit me on Monday. I didn't say anything then, and you might wonder why."

Everyone listens intently, silence enveloping the room.

Yes, even I want to know the reason, Clover thinks. *Why didn't you do anything then?*

"I was waiting for the right moment, and this, my friends, is that moment." Rodney spreads his arms. "I'm going to show this girly boy his place." He kneels beside Clover. "Look, everyone. Two smacks, and this thing can't even get up. What should I do?"

"Leave him, Rodney. He's too weak," one voice suggests.

Clover feels relief at the compassion shown by some of Rodney's friends.

"No, are you mad?" another says. "Make sure he learns his lesson. One more, Rodney."

"Yeah, one more," Rina concurs.

"All right! All right! If you say so." Rodney bends down, grips Clover's hair, and delivers a hit to his groin with his knee.

Clover's cry pierces the air—shrill, nerve-wracking, and haunting.

Rodney releases Clover's hair and leans over him again. "What are you crying for, eh?" Clover's face bathes in saline cascades. He turns his head, unable to express his agony. "Yeah? Really, it pains." Rodney scoffs. "It shouldn't, though. You haven't even got anything there. What did I hit? A toe?"

Amid the crowd's jubilant laughter, Clover remains tethered to the ground. The weight of his physical agony and discomfiture does not let him rise. Gradually, the room empties. He watches Rina abscond with the teddy bear—his teddy bear.

Time drags on interminably as Clover slowly pulls himself upright, limping toward his closet, where a mirror hangs. He stands before it, his reflection as grimy as the glass; his insides want to cry out loud. He examines his cheeks up close, bruised and painful, the rest of his face as red as an angry sunset, his under-eyes dusky orbits.

He cries not from being beaten, but because the fleeting charm of the day has vanished into oblivion.

Clover had been happy all day. He thinks of Ethan, presumably at home now, enjoying countless luxuries, a feast fit for a king, without a trace of concern. He doesn't fear being hurt. Clover is certain no one awaits him at home with such treatment. Yet here he is, confronted by an entirely divergent destiny, greeted by tormentors, enduring punches as if they were mere snacks, now engulfed in pain as he drifts into sleep. His lips release muted cries before finally succumbing to slumber.

The following day, Clover wakes up pining for food. He went to bed on an empty stomach and in pain. Every tendon and muscle in his body aches, including his pelvis. He sluggishly gets up, worried he will be late for school. The sun is already rising, but then it strikes him: it's the weekend. No school today. No school for the next two days.

He drops to the floor, releasing a painful sigh. He won't see his friend today, but he realizes it's for the best. For the first time, he is thankful that Rodney buffeted him on a Friday, sparing him from taking his marred face outside. And the best part is, he doesn't have to explain anything to Ethan, provided his bruises dissolve into memory before Monday.

A warm bath helps Clover. He thinks of visiting the clinic. *I need a painkiller. I hope it kills all my pain forever,* he thinks. He heads downstairs to the clinic, where Mrs. Wringer sits.

"Clover, my dear." Mrs. Wringer flies out of her chair as he enters. "What happened to you?"

Clover flings his arms around her timeworn legs and sobs in a muted way. She smells of oranges. His mouth waters. *She must have just come back from the kitchen,* he thinks.

Pulling away, he looks up at her. "Can you give me a painkiller, Mrs. Wringer?"

She nods. "Of course, but you have to tell me what happened. Did you fall?" She fills a medication cup with liquid, bringing it to his lips. "Here, take it."

It tastes medicinal, not as flavorful as the hospital one, with no trace of cherry at all. Clover wants to tell her to stock cherry-flavored medicine, but he knows his wish will never be granted.

"I ask again." Mrs. Wringer tosses the cup in the bin. "Tell me what happened."

Clover hesitates, fearing Rodney will find out, but feels he should be punished equally. Then it dawns on him that he was the one who started the row. He wouldn't have faced Rodney's wrath yesterday if he hadn't hit him on Monday. If he tells Mrs. Wringer about yesterday, he'll also have to explain what happened on Monday.

"I fell," Clover says. "Fell off the stairs."

"Hmm." Mrs. Wringer remains doubtful. "That bruise says otherwise. Did you get into a fight?"

"No, Mrs. Wringer. I did not." Clover looks down.

"Very well, then." She refrains from asking more questions and pats him on the back. "Go have breakfast, then lie down in your room."

* * *

It's Monday morning. Clover stands in front of the mirror again. The bruise hasn't faded much despite his continuous efforts. He has iced it so much that he can't feel half his face, sinew locked in frost. It was a rough weekend for Clover, a hellish ordeal. He stayed holed up in his room, only stepping out for meals. Rodney and his crew were kept at bay. Clover thinks Rodney has punished him enough.

His bruised and swollen face makes moving his mouth painful. A teardrop slips from his eye, and staying put seems sensible. But against that wisdom, he chooses to go to school.

Clover's journey feels unusually burdened today. His mind races, concocting false narratives to conceal the truth about the palette of contusions' hues. Each step on the pavement adds heft to the fabricated story he plans to tell Ethan. *I fell off the stairs, four in a row,* Clover rehearses quietly. *No, wait, at least seven. Yeah, that sounds... convincing.*

Yet, try as he might to steady his thoughts, memories of the tumultuous weekend storm his mind—the prodding from Rodney, the clash, and the fray that followed. His body feels a constant pang, and he dreads meeting Ethan.

As he approaches the school gates, Clover tries to smile, but it hurts. He proceeds to his classroom. Ethan isn't there yet. Clover takes his seat in the corner, concealing his battered cheek out of embarrassment.

"Hey!" Ethan enters and drops his bag. "How was your weekend?" He settles into his seat.

If there's anything close to hell, it was last weekend, Clover thinks. "It was okay," he replies quietly.

Ethan slides his lunchbox under the desk. "We went to Kamloops. Just Dad and me. Mom wouldn't come. She's sick again. Oh well." Ethan shrugs. "On Friday evening, after I got home, Dad suggested a road trip, and I said, why not?"

Clover gives him a fair ear, his attention finely tuned. "So, where is this place?"

Ethan looks at him. "Oh, Kamloops?"

Clover nods.

Ethan flings his hands upward. "Oh, I never told you!" He shakes his head. "I was born in Kamloops and just moved to Nelson last month."

"I didn't know," Clover says.

"Now you know! Dad drove for six hours," Ethan continues, "and we stopped twice. When we got there, Grandma was really happy to see us. She was glad Mom didn't come." He pauses, catching his breath, as if he has rehearsed this whole script. "Then she made—"

"Do you have a grandma?" Clover interrupts, uninterested in what she made. He doesn't want his mouth to water hearing about dishes he has never tasted.

"Yeah." Ethan nods slowly. "She has a problem, though. Dad says it's getting worse. She doesn't remember much. Alzheimer's, I think."

"I've never heard of it. What is it?"

"Umm... Dad told me Grandma is forgetful now. Old people usually have it. Does your grandma have it too?"

Clover's heart stalls. *I dunno,* he thinks, but remains silent.

Ethan studies him. "Hello?" he says, waving his hand in front of Clover's eyes. "Are you awake?"

Clover returns from the stupor, throws a tight-lipped smile, and turns to look outside. "I don't have a grandma."

Ethan bites his lip. *I shouldn't have asked him that,* he thinks. Not everyone has grandparents. He believes Clover misses his deceased grandparents. Little does he fathom that there is not a trace of Clover's parents, let alone his grandparents. "Sorry," Ethan says, tugging at his earlobe.

Clover turns back, momentarily forgetting his bruise. "It's okay."

Yet Ethan notices. He inches forward and asks, "What happened to your face?"

Clover's heart quickens, and he swiftly turns away.

Ethan tilts his head. "What's that bruise? Did someone hit you?"

His suspicions are accurate.

But Clover doesn't have the heart to tell him. "No, no. Er... I fell down the stairs—seven steps—and my face hit the railing... on Friday."

Ethan gasps. "Did you see a doctor?"

"Yeah, nothing to worry about. She gave me some painkillers."

Ethan seems almost convinced, so Clover hopes he won't pry further.

"Oh, good," Ethan says, releasing a sharp exhale.

Clover stays in his corner until the recess bell finally rings. After sharing lunch with Ethan, they wander beyond the school walls into the sun-drenched day, a gentle breeze swaying around them. Sitting on a bench, they watch other children play on the slides. But Clover is focused on nursing his tender cheek.

Ethan notices Clover touching his cheek. "It hurts, doesn't it?"

"Yeah." His accord accompanies a quiet nod.

"I meant to ask you." Ethan looks at Clover. "Would you like to come to my house today?"

Clover is stunned. Did he hear that correctly? Ethan is inviting him to visit. Despite the excitement bubbling within, Clover tries to mask it. "Why?" he questions, sounding disinterested.

"Because you're my friend. Aren't you?" Ethan furrows his brow.

Clover blushes slightly. "I am, yes."

"Then what's the problem?"

What if he insists on coming to my place? Clover worries. *I've been lying to him about my parents and my house. What if he ends our friendship because I'm a liar? No, no. I can't let this happen.*

"What's wrong, Clover?" Ethan asks, puzzled by his silence. It shouldn't take much thought to visit a friend's house.

"I can't come." Clover drops his shoulders, sighing.

Ethan jumps to his feet, shocked. "Why?"

Clover bows his head, needing an excuse. "My parents won't agree," he says.

"What do you mean they won't agree? They let you roam the streets alone. Why wouldn't they let you come over?"

Clover's lack of response corroborates Ethan's point. He is right. If his parents let him out on his own, what problem could they possibly have with him visiting Ethan's house?

"Please, Clover." Ethan keeps his hand on his knee. "Come over. I promise my parents won't mind. Dad is really nice. He loves children. Mom is a bit weird, but I know she'll be happy to see you."

A soft breath of wind runs through Clover's hair as he keeps his head lowered in profound thought. After a moment of contemplation, he looks at Ethan and says, "Okay, I'll come with you."

Ethan's heart teems with joy as he leaps into the air, a broad smile lighting up his face like the afternoon sun. He is thrilled that his best friend has agreed to visit his house, excited for school-day constraints to dissolve into endless playtime. Clover joins in the celebration, enticed by the prospect of hours spent together—unfettered by schedules and bullies. He cannot deny the allure, even if his imaginary parents would disapprove. But at that moment, he doesn't care.

Ten

∞

VISIT TO VERDI MANSION

Recess is over, and Ethan and Clover can hardly sit still, eagerly awaiting the end of classes. When the bell rings, they hop outside, Clover following closely behind, thinking about the luxury car he will ride in for the first time. There it is, parked right outside the gate, with Mr. Manson holding the door open, ready for the boys to jump inside.

"Hey!" Mr. Manson grips Clover's arm, stopping him from entering the car. "Where do you think you're going?"

Clover does not answer and looks at Ethan to intervene.

"Mr. Manson," Ethan scoffs, "he's my friend and is coming to Verdi Mansion with us."

Mr. Manson releases Clover's arm, nods slightly, and takes his seat in the front.

Clover remains standing outside, flustered, with his hands folded together. His inner voice warns him against going. *You don't belong there. They are rich, and you are poor. Stop, Clover. Don't go. Just don't.*

Ethan realizes the gravity of Mr. Manson's words, which have shattered Clover's lively spirit and made him feel inferior. Clover thinks he isn't fit to sit in the car, but Ethan trusts Mr. Manson needn't have taken that path.

"It would have been better if you hadn't stopped him like that," he tells Mr. Manson angrily. Then he steps out and takes Clover's arms. "Sorry about him, Clover. Come on."

"I think I should go home," Clover says, abandoning his enthusiastic plans like leaves falling from a forgotten autumn tree.

"Don't be silly." Ethan tugs him closer and helps him into the seat.

Clover feels a little better but notices Mr. Manson glancing at him through the rearview mirror. Nervously, he looks around. The car's interior feels like stepping into another world, with elegance and sophistication at its peak. The leather seats are like plump clouds, hugging his body as he sinks into the bolster. There are numerous buttons gleaming on the dial and armrest, and a scent of novelty—perhaps just the air freshener—fills the air, a blend of leather, pine, and wood.

As Mr. Manson starts driving, the engine hums softly, as quiet as a whisper. Clover's stomach growls louder than the engine at times. In awe, he peers outside, taking in the swift movement of Nelson—the shops, the bakeries. To his right lies the orphanage, a sight he consciously avoids, especially in this fleeting moment.

As they drive through the busy market, their trajectory shifts toward the residential area, where the houses stand in uniformity, resembling a world of doppelgängers. Clover wonders if people ever stray and end up in a different house. Perhaps there's a system to tell them apart, so he asks Ethan, "How do you tell which is yours? They all look the same."

Ethan giggles.

Mr. Manson hears him and snorts.

"They are numbered," Ethan explains. "Each house has a number."

"I see." Clover didn't know that; it was certainly a piece of information he was oblivious to.

"Don't you have a house?" Ethan asks out of curiosity. "It should have a house number."

Clover delves into thought again. *Does Whispering Hearts have a number?* He doesn't know. "I don't think so," he whispers.

Ethan sighs and shakes his head. "I'll visit your house one day and show you where it usually is."

Clover presses his lips together, his breath caught in his throat. He refrains from answering. Of course, he doesn't want his best friend to visit his house. *Because it's not my house.* He stays silent and gazes outside again.

With a subsequent right turn, they enter a quieter enclave where the residences swell in grandeur and stature. Clover's eyes widen with wonder as he beholds these structures. He has never been to this side of Nelson. *Maybe only the rich live here,* he thinks, and he is right in his assumptions. The colossal houses boast wealth; their front yards bathe in opulence with multihued plants. The driveways shine like burnished metal, where the vehicles of pomp are parked.

Mr. Manson veers onto a trail leading to a mansion guarded by iron gates that are already open. He stops the vehicle at the entrance, where the house resembles a cathedral. Clover's assumptions are confirmed: Ethan's house is far grander than his orphanage. His humble dwelling cannot compare to the estate before him—a mansion so vast that it eclipses Clover's wildest dreams.

Mr. Manson turns to the boys. "Here we are, boys." He steps out of the vehicle and opens the door for Ethan. "Please go straight inside. Mrs. Verdi should be home. I have to pick up Mr. Verdi."

"Okay," Ethan says as he exits the car.

Clover slides to Ethan's side and jumps out. Ethan takes his hand staunchly, and together they ascend to the entryway.

Clover looks at the convoluted railing with its various patterns, unlike the rusty iron railing at his orphanage. Touching the latter would often leave his hands coated in brown, with remnants of rust lingering on his skin and a metallic scent filling his nostrils.

The mansion's entrance is guarded by an oak door crafted from polished mahogany, deep and rich in color, with handles bearing elaborate Baroque designs. The gigantic doorway swings open, revealing a vast foyer. The ceilings stretch high above. A man garbed in a gray uniform welcomes them inside, bestowing a deferential bow upon Ethan and offering a cursory greeting to Clover, whose curious eyes scan the surroundings with muted fascination.

Clover's "hello" goes unheard, as the man continues to eye him warily, perceiving him as a street urchin due to his clothing.

Ethan hands over his school bag to the man and orchestrates a run through the palatial space. Beyond the foyer is a sweeping staircase, bedecked in red velvet and floral motifs, ascending to the second floor. Ethan nearly runs up the stairs, with Clover struggling to keep pace.

"Come on. I'll show you my room." Ethan turns to his left.

On the second floor, Clover takes in the extravagance slowly. The red carpet continues along the corridor. Ethan halts before a door and waves his hand, beckoning Clover to hurry. "Come on, fast."

Clover dashes forward. As the door swings open at Ethan's touch, his eyes widen at the sight of the magnificent room. His attention is immediately drawn to the colossal bed, its resplendence evident in its vastness and the plush velour covering the headboard. How wonderful it must be to rest his head against such a cushiony surface—so different from the wall he has as a headboard.

The room is a constellation of lights embedded in the ceiling, making it bright. Clover cannot help but compare it to the lighting in his room, which is yellow, morbid, and depressing. Sometimes the bulb would go out, and no one would replace it for days, leaving him to yield to the darkness at night.

His gaze flits from one corner to another. A plethora of toys occupies one corner, a kingdom of whimsy waiting to be explored. Cars, train sets, plush toys—he has it all. The sheer abundance overwhelms Clover.

Adjacent to this playful corner is another world: a study area with shelves filled with books. Clover wonders why Ethan has so many books when he cannot read properly. He refrains from asking, but he knows he would love to sit in this corner, reading books filled with pictures, illustrations, and colors all day.

The upholstery flows effortlessly over the settees and chairs. Clover marvels at their number, wondering why one would need so many seats. A child like Ethan would only need a bed. There are also vast, billowing drapes wrapping the windows in layers of ivory. Sunlight streams into the room, casting a spotlight on the center of the bed.

Clover walks toward the window, where a vast garden spreads out before him. It looks like a nursery, bursting with color against an emerald backdrop, while swings sway gently in the breeze.

"Do you have swings and slides in your garden?" Clover whispers. "Wow!"

"What did you say?" Ethan asks.

Clover's mouth hangs open as he struggles to grasp the reality before him. Beyond the garden lies a shimmering pool, a cerulean gem amidst the greenery. The water ripples across the surface, glistening in the sunlight.

Clover wants to stay by the pool. It's not too deep like the lake; he is afraid of the lake's depth and would never go in unless absolutely necessary. But the pool is different—it's shallow. *Maybe I can,* he thinks, *but I don't know.*

Dizzy with disbelief, Clover feels awe, wonder, and a tinge of longing. It's a world far beyond the scope of his imagination.

"Did you like my room?" Ethan asks.

Clover looks at him, noticing his innocent smile. A part of him wants to respond: *What kind of stupid question is that? Your room is grand, and there's no reason for me not to like it.*

"Of course," he replies quietly, smiling.

Ethan leaps onto his bed; it emits no squeaks. It looks like a soft, inviting surface. "Come here, Clover."

Clover hesitantly perches on the corner, sinking into the mattress—quicker than quicksand—but he knows he won't be trapped. He likes it.

"Not in the corner, Clover," Ethan exhales. "Come here." He taps the mattress, inviting him over.

Clover removes his shoes and climbs onto the bed. Ethan still has his shoes on, but Clover fears he might stain the sheets with dirt from outside. They trudge through dirt every day, yet Ethan seems unbothered.

"Um... maybe you should take off your shoes too," Clover suggests.

Ethan shrugs and ignores him. "I'm hungry. Do you want to play or eat first?"

Clover presses his lips together, unable to decide.

Ethan jumps to his feet. "Let's eat first."

Clover follows him down to the ground floor. Ethan leads him into the dining hall, where the dining table is so large it could seat all the children in the orphanage.

"How many people live in this house?" Clover cannot resist asking.

Ethan pulls out a chair for Clover. "Me, Mom, and Dad. And yes, there is staff."

"Why do you need such a big dining table?" Clover sits down, staring at the chandelier above, which casts a warm glow.

"Oh, I don't know." Ethan sits beside him, reaching for an apple artistically arranged in a golden fruit basket. "Do you want some?"

Clover shakes his head, though his mouth waters at the delightful crunch and juicy bursts as Ethan bites into the apple. He resists the temptation. He has often had apples, but he notices something different in the basket—a scaly, bright pink fruit resembling a pinecone.

"Do you eat that too?" he asks.

"What?" Ethan asks, his mouth full of apple, bits flying as he speaks.

"That pink-colored thing. Is that for decoration?"

"No." Ethan gulps. "That's dragon fruit."

Clover feels foolish. Of course there's fruit in a fruit basket. What else would it be? He sighs, exhaling his embarrassment.

Ethan places the apple core on a folded napkin near his plate. "Have some, Clover. But I don't know how to cut it. Ms. Imelda!" he calls.

A short young woman with long, curly hair appears at the table, carrying two large pots. "Yes, sir." She sets them down and wipes her hands on her apron, which hangs over her black skirt. "How can I help?" She smiles at Ethan, fluttering her thick eyelashes.

Clover flicks a glance at the pots, noticing steam rising from them. They smell of vegetables.

"Can you cut the dragon fruit for Clover?" Ethan asks.

"Of course, sir," Imelda replies at once. She scurries to the kitchen and returns with a knife, slicing open the exotic fruit to reveal its polka-dotted white flesh. Her small fingers, nails like pinpricks, deftly carve it into cubes, which she arranges neatly on a plate before presenting it to Clover.

Clover eagerly pops a cube into his mouth. The sweet, tangy flavor bursts across his tongue—unlike anything he has ever tasted. He quickly finishes the serving, while Ethan watches him with delight.

Imelda then places a bowl in front of them and pours steaming soup from one of the pots. Clover studies it: assorted vegetables floating in a brown broth—cubes of white, green, orange, and red.

They savor the soup, but Clover soon feels full. He starts to rise, but Ethan stops him.

"What's wrong? Where are you going?"

"Um…" Clover sits back down. "We're done, right?"

"What?" Ethan laughs. "No, silly. That was just an appetizer. The main course is still coming."

Clover finds this strange. At the orphanage, when they have stew, it is usually just stew—and sometimes a slice of bread.

He sits quietly as Imelda returns, placing before them a beautifully seared fillet of sablefish, its ember-bronzed surface scored with flame-kissed lines, resting in a pool of golden sauce. Velvety morel mushrooms follow, nestled around the fish, along with delicate herbs and sauces layered with unfamiliar richness.

Ethan unfolds a golden linen napkin, tucks it into his collar, and reaches for the silverware—knife in one hand and fork in the other—using them with perfect coordination to slice through the fish, steadying the succulent piece with his fork.

Clover tries to mimic him but is abruptly stopped just as he is about to take a bite of the soft black cod.

"Wait," Ethan halts him. "You're not allergic to fish, are you?"

Clover shrugs, his mouth downturned. "I don't know. I've never had this dish before."

Ethan nods. "Okay. Sorry. Go ahead."

Clover enjoys the fish—the sauces, the mushrooms, the herbs. It's beyond delicious, and he feels beyond full.

"One more bite and my stomach will explode," he tells Ethan.

Ethan laughs and sets his cutlery down. "I'm full too. Let's go see Mom."

"Okay."

Clover follows Ethan, who takes a different route along the ground floor. He swerves left, then right, and then left again until he stops before a door.

"Mom!" He knocks. "Mom!"

No answer. Clover notices Ethan's nervousness.

"I—I don't know why she isn't opening the door. Maybe she's asleep."

They almost begin to walk away when the door opens, and a woman's voice calls out.

"Ethan?"

"Mom!" Ethan turns and rushes toward a frail woman in a cotton nightgown.

Samantha Verdi, tying her thin, unkempt hair into a low bun, steps forward, her eyes clouded as she looks at Clover.

"Who's that, Ethan?" Her voice is soft yet frayed.

"My friend, Mom." Ethan gestures toward Clover. "Come!"

Clover approaches them slowly, his heart pounding for reasons he doesn't fully understand. He bows slightly in greeting.

"Hello, Mrs. Verdi."

Samantha shudders, taking Clover's hands, touching his ears, and looking into his eyes. "Who are you?"

Clover steps back, confused. "I—I... sorry?"

Ethan discreetly smacks his forehead. "He is my friend. I told you."

Samantha raises her hand to silence Ethan, crouching down to hold Clover's arm. "What's your name?" Her mouth drops open, and her eyes widen. "Where are you from?"

She notices the bruise on his cheek and brushes it softly with her fingers. "What happened to your cheek?"

Clover gulps, his heart racing, but he sees a strange sadness in her eyes —the way she looks at him, her grasp as if she would never let him go.

"I'm Clover Nelson, Mrs. Verdi. My cheek... I fell off the stairs."

"Does it hurt?" Samantha asks, her eyes unblinking, her dry lips oozing blood.

Clover looks at Ethan. "I'm fine, Mrs. Verdi. Totally fine."

Samantha looks at Clover as if he were a beautiful painting in human form. "Where do you live?"

Ethan, confused, interrupts. "Mom, why are you asking him so many questions?"

"Your ears..." Samantha murmurs, then asks again, "Where do you live?"

"In—in Nelson," Clover says.

"In Nelson," Samantha whispers, looking at Clover steadily. "Tell me your parents' names."

Clover swallows hard. *I must make up some names.* "Matthew Nelson and Marina Nelson."

He doesn't know where those names come from, but he's relieved they came to him.

Samantha lets out a heavy sigh, her shoulders sagging. "Okay, so you really are Clover."

A shiver runs down Clover's spine. "Who did you think I was?"

Samantha looks at him, her gaze shifting from his ears to his eyes. "No one," she says—then seems to drift off, her mouth open, eyes staring blankly at the marble floor.

"Mrs. Verdi?" Clover gently places his hand on her shoulder.

Samantha startles. "Huh? What?"

Clover hides behind Ethan.

Samantha stands up, looking at Ethan. "Did you eat? Both of you?"

"Yes," Ethan replies, trying to ease his furrowed brow.

"Okay, good." Samantha steps back, her head swaying gently. "I must find him," she whispers, retreating into her room and closing the door.

Ethan watches his mother disappear into her den of reclusion, his eyes welling with tears, his heart aching for motherly love—but Samantha is lost in her own world.

The grand bed calls to Samantha, and she sprawls across it again, muttering under her breath. "Where is he? He must be here. I have to go out and find him." Then she pulls the blanket over herself and closes her eyes.

Ethan feels weak, his knees trembling, his nose tinged red, its openings constantly flaring as he battles to hold back the flow of tears about to escape.

"Is Mrs. Verdi sick?" Clover asks, placing a hand on Ethan's shoulder.

Ethan shakes his head vigorously and strides out of the hall.

Clover, sensing Ethan's pain, follows him. "Wait, Ethan."

Ethan stops in the foyer, pressing his hand against his chest, trying to slow his breath, wiping his dewy eyes.

Clover rushes into the foyer.

"Are you ready to play?" Ethan forces a smile. "Let's go in the garden."

Clover feels bad for him. He holds Ethan's arm and says, "It's okay if your mother is sick. You don't need to feel embarrassed."

Tears brim in Ethan's eyes. No matter how hard he tries to hold them back, he bursts into sobs, unable to contain himself.

"Did you see her?" he cries. "She is like a walking ghost and doesn't care if I exist. She never eats with me, never plays with me. I'm always alone." He whimpers. "I hate having her as my mother. She is the worst."

Clover wraps him in a hug. "It's okay. She'll be fine soon."

"I don't know. I've never seen her fine." Ethan snuffles. "Dad is good, but she is just—"

"Ethan?"

A deep, commanding voice seems to emanate from nowhere and everywhere at once. Robert Verdi enters, standing behind Clover.

"What happened to you?" he asks.

Ethan pulls away from Clover and runs into his father's arms. "Dad!"

Clover watches as Robert, tall and dashing in his tuxedo, lifts Ethan with affection.

"What's wrong, son? Tell me."

"Mom. She is sick again," Ethan says. "I took my friend to meet her." He points to Clover. "And then she asked some strange questions and went into her room." He clings to Robert's neck, whispering, "I'm so embarrassed."

"Don't worry." Robert sets him down. "I'll take her to the doctor."

Clover, feeling shy and curling up in a corner, catches Robert's eye.

"Meanwhile, why don't you introduce me to your friend?"

"Yes, of course, Dad." Ethan snuffles. "This is Clover, my friend from school."

Robert's smile dissolves into the ether. He becomes wary, a frown forming on his forehead.

"Are you really?"

Clover's gaze fixates on Robert's lips, which move with words uncaught, lost like vapors in the wind. "I didn't catch that."

Robert reacts similarly to Samantha, though less intensely. "Where do you live, Clover?" he asks, his brow raised.

"In Nelson. My parents are Matthew and Marina Nelson." Clover repeats what he told Samantha, puzzled that they both asked the same question.

"Okay." Robert nods, his lips forming a wry crescent. Clover senses he may not be convinced by his fabricated identity.

"Bring your parents someday, all right?" Robert says. "I'd like to meet them."

"Yes," Ethan adds. "Bring your parents, Clover. We'll have dinner together." He looks at Robert. "But what about Mom?"

"Don't worry about her, Ethan." Robert pats his head. "I'll take care of her."

Clover bows as Robert whips past them. *Why do you want to meet my parents?* A sudden desire to vanish gnaws at him. "I want to go home, Ethan." He wraps his arms around himself, feeling out of place in the mansion and overwhelmed by their questions.

"Already?" Ethan throws his hands in the air. "But why?"

Clover remains silent but thinks, *Why are they both so interested in my parents? Do they not want Ethan to be friends with me?*

"We haven't even played yet," Ethan protests, clearly upset by the idea. "The whole plan was to play for as long as we wanted." Then it dawns on him. "Is it because of my mom?"

"No," Clover says. "My parents will be waiting for me. I didn't tell them I was coming here, so I should go."

I know it's because of Mom.

"Okay, then," Ethan says sadly. "I'll come to drop you off."

"No," Clover insists. "If my parents see you anywhere near my house, they'll be upset."

"Why? That's so stupid," Ethan retorts, crossing his arms.

"I know, but my parents are a little strange. If Mr. Manson can drop me off at the market, I can walk home from there. You stay with your dad."

Ethan affirms with a tilt of his head. "All right." He ushers Clover outside, then conveys his request to Mr. Manson.

Mr. Manson agrees.

Clover sits in the car. "Thank you."

"Bye, Clover." Ethan waves, sadness in his eyes. "See you tomorrow at school."

"Bye, Ethan." Clover waves back.

Mr. Manson drives Clover back to his reality, leaving behind the scenery of luxurious homes, with the sun setting and the amber mountains telling the tale of a day fading away.

The main market comes into view. "Can you stop here, please?" Clover asks, realizing they've reached his destination.

"Here?" Mr. Manson halts the car near the curb, twists his neck, and looks back at Clover, who is curled up in the back seat. "Is your house in the main market?"

"No, sir, but I'll manage," Clover says timidly. "Walking every day is normal for me."

Mr. Manson arches his eyebrows, then lowers them quickly. "Fine. You can step out, boy."

Clover exits the car, carefully closing the door behind him. "Thank you, Mr. Manson."

Mr. Manson doesn't respond, rolling up his window and driving away.

Clover begins his solitary journey. His feet feel heavy, burdened by the untruths he has spun for Ethan. He thinks about Ethan's grand house, his bedroom, his garden—things Clover can only dream of. He cannot deny the incongruity of Ethan's parents' probing questions, as if they had glimpsed a part of his life he keeps hidden.

With his mind wrestling with thoughts, he returns to his dormitory and sits by the window in quiet contemplation until the sun's last beam departs, giving way to the arrival of twilight.

Eleven

FINDING CLOVER'S PARENTS

"Hey!" Ethan calls out as he enters the school grounds through the gate, walking alongside Clover, who has just arrived. "Were your parents okay? Did they get upset with you?"

Clover struggles to respond. No one at the orphanage worries about where he goes; it only becomes a concern at night—especially for Agatha. He shakes his head, a gesture meant to avoid lying.

They enter their classroom, and a heaviness settles in Clover's chest. The burden of his lies has stolen his smile today. As he considers revealing his hidden reality, he weighs the consequences. Would he lose his friend if he told the truth?

He knows, however, that the truth will come out eventually. One day, Ethan will discover that Clover is an orphan—an unworthy friend—and on that day, his parents will forbid him from speaking to Clover again. He fears that moment. After so long, he has finally found a friend, and he is loath to lose him.

He has so much to say, yet he remains silent, stealing glances at Ethan during class. He thinks that Ethan, too, is suffering—just in a different way. His mother has brought him sorrow, but at least he has a father who loves him. He has access to the world's luxuries. *How bad can it be to live with an incompetent mother?* Clover wonders bitterly. *I've lived without one.*

Throughout the lessons, Clover wrestles with conflicting thoughts, questioning whether his deception is a benevolent lie or a wall standing between true friendship.

During recess, they sit together on a bench in the playground. Clover is almost ready—*almost*—to unburden himself and bare his soul, but Ethan speaks first.

"Can I come to your house today?"

Clover's heart sinks. His hands tremble. There is no way he can take Ethan home. He stands at the brink of revelation, exhaustion pressing down on him. He cannot carry the lie any longer.

If Ethan ends our friendship after this, he thinks, *so be it. This lie protected me once—but now it's suffocating. I want to be free.*

"No," he replies quietly.

"Rude," Ethan frowns. "Why not? I took you to my house yesterday."

Clover looks at him with a hangdog expression. "Thank you for that. But I can't take you to mine."

"Why not?" Ethan's voice rises.

Clover lowers his head, his face like a wilted bloom. "Because I've been lying to you."

Ethan slowly rises from the bench. "Lying to me about what?"

Clover meets his baffled stare. "About everything."

Ethan's mind races, trying to assemble the pieces of Clover's puzzle. Then—suddenly—it clicks.

"Your parents aren't good people, are they?" Ethan says carefully. "They hurt you, and you're embarrassed to tell me. That's why you don't want me to visit your house. Am I right?"

Clover gives a silent nod.

Ethan drops beside him with a dull thud. "I knew it." He sighs and pats Clover's shoulder. "I feel sorry for you. But you know... one day you'll leave that place and live on your own."

Clover shakes his head. "I've been living on my own for a long time, Ethan."

Ethan tilts his head. "What do you mean?"

Clover exhales slowly, as if letting something fragile slip free. "I don't have parents, Ethan. I live at Whispering Hearts Orphanage. My parents left me when I was eight months old."

Ethan blinks. "What's an... or—orphanage?"

Clover stares at him, stunned that something so central to his existence could be unknown. "An orphanage is a place where children without parents are raised," he says quietly.

Ethan smacks his forehead. "Are you serious?" He hesitates. "Are they... dead?"

Clover shrugs. "I don't know."

Ethan stands again, pacing in tight, restless loops. "Why didn't you tell me before?"

Clover says nothing.

"Why, Clover?"

"Because I thought you wouldn't want to be friends with me," Clover admits. "If you knew I wasn't rich like you—and that I don't have parents —you'd want another friend. Someone more like yourself."

Ethan stops pacing. "Did you really think that?" He shakes his head, frustration and regret tangled together. "I knew something was off. I noticed when you didn't bring lunch. When your clothes and shoes looked worn. Your parents—well, the way you talked about them— didn't make sense. They didn't take care of you." He looks at Clover, softer now. "Now that I know you don't have parents... I'm actually relieved."

"Relieved?" Clover asks. "How can you say that?"

Ethan sits again. "Because at least it explains things. Having bad parents isn't a reason. This is."

Clover's voice cracks. "Having no parents *is* the reason. And it's hard. Cruel, sometimes. You'll never understand."

Ethan swallows. "I'm sorry, Clover."

Clover doesn't look at him, but he nods.

Ethan leans closer, studying the bruise on Clover's cheek. "You didn't get that falling down the stairs, did you?" His voice hardens. "Someone hit you."

Clover dips his head in confirmation.

"Do people hit kids in orphanages?" Ethan asks carefully. "Does everyone get hit?"

"No," Clover says. "Kids don't get hit. It's just me. I'm an easy target. There's an older boy who bullies me. Sometimes he beats me up."

"Why?" Ethan asks.

"He doesn't like me," Clover says. "I don't know any other reason."

Ethan draws in a sharp breath. "That's not okay. Did you tell anyone?"

Clover shakes his head. "No one does anything."

"Do you want my dad to talk to the people at your orphanage? He can surely fix things. They seem bad."

"No, please." Clover clasps his hands together in a plea. "I don't want your parents to know I'm an orphan."

"Why not?" Ethan asks. "What will they say? You're still worried about my mom, right?"

"No. I just know they won't let you be friends with me." Clover rises to his feet. "Didn't you notice how they asked me about my parents?"

"So what? It doesn't matter."

"It does," Clover insists. "It matters to your parents. I'm glad it doesn't matter to you."

Ethan looks at Clover and says dolefully, "Okay, Clover. I won't tell my parents about you—ever."

"Promise?" Clover extends his cupped palm.

Ethan takes his hand. "Promise."

The two embrace, and Clover feels on the verge of tears, grateful to have a friend like Ethan. Maybe that's exactly what friends should be.

"Clover!" Ethan pulls away. "Do you even know who your parents are?"

Clover shakes his head. "No idea."

"Have you ever asked—umm—the people at your orphanage? Who dropped you off? Was there a letter?"

The thought had crossed Clover's mind before. He recalls asking Agatha about his parents and her vague reply: *I don't know who dropped you off. Just know they did not want you and have a reason for it.*

"Ms. Preen doesn't know," he says.

"How can she not know?"

"Because she told me."

"And you believed her? That's silly." Ethan is surprised by Clover's lack of persistence. "She would have some information about you."

Clover furrows his brows. "How can you be so sure?"

"Because I know." Ethan rolls his eyes. "You should find out, too. It's just—so weird that you don't even know who your parents are, who dropped you off, or if they are even—"

"I get it," Clover interrupts. "You're right."

A new desire to uncover the truth stirs in Clover's heart. He agrees with Ethan; nothing he said was wrong. He should have tried harder. But his fear of Agatha has always overshadowed his desire to know who he really is.

He is content with what fate has given him, but listening to Ethan, his curiosity ignites, and he promises to begin the quest to fathom his life's divergent path. "I'll ask Ms. Preen tonight."

"Good." Ethan boosts his confidence. "If she doesn't tell you, then find out yourself."

"And how should I do that?"

"Let me tell you." Ethan tilts his head, his voice almost a whisper. Clover has to press his ear close. "I know the offices have a lot of papers— in bins, cabinets, under the desk—everywhere. My dad has some, too. You'll find something in those documents."

Clover covers his mouth in shock. *Why didn't I think of that?*

"My dad calls me little Sheblock," Ethan says, puffing up with pride. "I'm very good at finding things out."

"A Sheblock? What's that?" Clover asks, confused.

"He is a detec—detec...sive. Yeah, that."

"Detective," Clover corrects him. "And I think you're talking about Sherlock, not Sheblock."

"Yes, exactly. That's how my dad says it." Ethan huffs. "I'm just a kid. Don't expect me to say all the words right. I'm still learning."

Clover releases a merry laugh, his heart swelling with fondness for Ethan, who, at that moment, feels more like a brother than just a friend.

"So, will you do it tonight?" Ethan asks.

"Yeah." Clover nods.

The bell rings, signaling the end of recess. The students begin to gather indoors, and together they head to their remaining lessons.

Later that afternoon, Clover arrives at the orphanage. He considers going directly to Agatha, so he knocks on the door with his bag still slung over his shoulder.

Agatha sounds agitated as usual. "Who is it?"

Clover hesitates. He dislikes her tone when she is calm, let alone when she is angry. *What could it be this time?* Valiantly, as if entering a war zone, he pushes the door open and peeks inside. Agatha rests her head on the table, unaware of his presence. A large amber bottle lies next to her. Clover isn't sure what it is. *Surely some delicious drink,* he thinks.

He tiptoes closer, leaning in to see if she is asleep. "Ms. Preen?" he calls quietly.

Agatha lifts her head, her eyes stormy, as if about to unleash her anger. Her blood-red lipstick smudges across her mouth, and her hair is a tangled mess. "Clover, is that you?" she asks. "What are you doing here?"

Clover steps back in fear, having never seen her in such disarray. After a brief pause, he gathers the courage to speak. "I—I want to ask you something, Ms. Preen." His heart flutters as he speaks.

"Go to the lake," she snaps. "I don't care if you're late. Stay there if you'd like."

She drops her head back onto the table wearily, her mouth open, her body slumping as if drained of all strength. Then she rallies again, picks up the amber bottle, raises it to her lips, but stops when she realizes the lid is still on. Irritated, she opens it forcefully, drops the lid to the ground, and gulps down whatever is inside.

The bottle now appears empty. Agatha has drained its contents, her tongue hovering at the rim, ready to catch the last drops should they descend along its desolate inner surface. A scant trickle egresses and lands on her tongue, and she closes her mouth, satisfied to have consumed the final drop.

She glances at Clover. "Why are you still here?" Her voice trembles.

Clover's heart races, but he steels himself to ask, "I want to know about my parents, Ms. Preen. Do you know them? Who are they, or who were they? Where did I come from?"

Agatha pouts her lips, resembling an intoxicated duck. Her eyes are red, and her fingers are interlaced as she opens her mouth to speak, but no words spill forth. Instead, she shrugs and leans back.

"Ms. Preen, please," Clover pleads. "I need to know. Please."

"What are you going to do about it? Your parents didn't want you. So here you are," she says.

"I know they didn't want me," he responds confidently, stirring Agatha from her languid posture. "Please tell me if they are still alive and where I came from."

Agatha props her head forward. "I gave you the surname you flaunt for a reason," she smirks. "You're Nelson's rat. Now, go away."

Clover's expression remains puzzled; he doesn't understand why she likens him to a rat.

Agatha closes her eyes again. Understanding the futility of inquiring further with her—aware she would tell him nothing—Clover retreats to his dormitory, biding his time until the sun crawls into darkness. At that point, he plans to undertake his mission to unearth the truth about his parents, anticipating that Agatha will likely be incapacitated in a few hours, allowing him the chance to stealthily infiltrate her office and scour through the papers, just like Sherlock, as Ethan suggested.

Today, he will discover the truth for himself—and for that, he needs the cover of night.

After supper, Clover dashes to his room, eagerly counting down the minutes to midnight, the perfect time to begin his investigation without the risk of being interrupted by anyone still awake. With an hour yet to pass, he battles drowsiness, struggling to keep his eyes open. Despite his overwhelming fatigue, he musters the strength to stand and heads to the restroom to dispel the weariness, splashing his face with cool water in hopes of banishing the final relics of sleep from his eyes.

With time still to spare before midnight, Clover decides to check if Agatha is asleep. He quietly makes his way to her office, standing at the door, his toes wiggling from anxiety. He pushes it ajar gingerly, the creaking sound making him pause to peer inside and see if she is truly sleeping. She must be; otherwise, the creaking would have alerted her by now.

He slips inside, barefoot, and quietly closes the door behind him. Agatha isn't there. He scans the room cautiously. His heart sinks at the thought of Agatha emerging from the shadows with a cane, ready to beat him. But he continues to the cabinet, relieved that she isn't present.

Clover moves cautiously in the darkness toward the cabinet he knows is there. He twists it open and feels what seems like a stack of files. In the maze of documents, he feels lost, unable to find what he seeks.

Moving to the window, he pulls back the curtain to let in a sliver of light. He brings the files closer to the window. He finds nothing. He grabs more files and scans them. Still nothing. Not a trace of his name. He sorts through them one by one but can't find anything.

Frustration mounts. He turns to Agatha's drawers. They are locked, another wall against his quest. He thinks hard, then decides to check the drawers beneath the cabinet, where a glimmer of hope emerges: folders neatly arranged in alphabetical order. He jumps to C, thinking they might be sorted by first names, but soon realizes they are arranged by surnames instead. He finds N.

But there is no child named Nelson. He feels appalled, unable to grasp why his identity is so mysterious. He considers giving up, but some inner voice urges him to continue searching through more folders. *My file could have been misplaced. Yes, that's a possibility,* he thinks.

An hour has passed. He has checked all the files from A to U, but there is no file there. No child with a surname starting with U lives at the orphanage.

With a heavy sigh, he shuts the drawer, feeling exasperated and angry. It feels as if he does not exist at all. *I know I am not Nelson. But am I not Clover?* he ponders. He has an identity that is deliberately concealed from everyone. A few tears escape his eyes, but he cannot allow himself to weaken now.

Just a few more files, and he'll be done. He wonders if it's worth his time. He has gone through most of them yet found nothing significant. But he presses on, determined to sift through the concluding bits of his probe, convinced he won't uncover anything.

It's V. He thinks of Ethan's surname, Verdi. What a sophisticated name he has. He opens the folder and finds two files, one belonging to Rodney Vaughn. He quickly opens his file, leaving the other on the floor without looking at the name, and discovers that Rodney's parents are dead. It doesn't specify how they died. Rodney was born in Surrey and dropped off at the orphanage by his aunt.

He reads his aunt's comments in his mind: *Due to my terminal cancer,*

I cannot raise Rodney anymore. I have no money to support him. Please take care of him.

For the first time, Clover feels sad for Rodney. He truly has no one in the world he can call his own. He wonders if Rodney knows his parents are gone. Perhaps he does, but pretends to be unaffected.

With a heavy sigh, he turns to the next file lying on the floor. The name reads: **Nathan Verdi.** A sinking feeling fills his chest. His feet feel numb; his hands tremble as he opens the file and reads:

Name: Nathan Verdi

Date of Birth: June 11, 1991

Dropped at the orphanage on: February 21, 1992

Current name: Clover Nelson

Clover's jaw drops. It's his file, and his real name is Nathan Verdi. He continues reading the notes:

Requested by the father to not go by his real name. Letter attached.

He notices a letter stapled to the page, folded many times into a small square. His heart beats faster than a drumroll as he unfolds the secrets contained in the letter.

Dear Orphanage Director,

With a heavy heart, I leave my son, Nathan Verdi, at your doorstep. Due to circumstances far beyond my control, I have decided to renounce my son. Let him be known as Clover. No one (I cannot stress this enough) can ever know his real identity. To ensure you comply with my directions, I'll send you money every month—more than you can imagine. But his real name must remain a secret.

Nathan should receive the highest standard of care. Provide him with a comfortable bed, good food, and clothes. He should never suffer. You can reach me at the phone number on the card if you need more money.

Enclosed are his birth certificate and medical reports. Nathan has Androgen Insensitivity Syndrome. He'll be abnormal forever.

All I ask is that you take good care of him.

Robert Verdi.

The file yields no birth certificate or medical reports, leaving Clover to wonder what exactly Robert meant by that term when he abandoned him. He checks the drawers again but finds nothing more, pondering whether Agatha has hidden it elsewhere or if there ever was a birth certificate.

Clover snaps the file shut, feeling as if the air has been sucked from the room. He stands frozen, unable to utter a word. His heart races with grief and pain as he absorbs the truth he has unearthed. His father's name, Robert Verdi, is the same as Ethan's.

The truth dawns with a jolt: he and Ethan share this name. *Our ears,* Clover thinks, touching his protruding ears. *They are so similar.* That must mean Ethan is my… brother.

Everything clicks into place. In a frenzy, Clover shoves the files back into the drawer and hurries out of Agatha's office, storming to his room and collapsing onto the bed. A muffled scream escapes his lips.

He dwells on Robert Verdi, the father who pledged comfort yet never delivered. No plush beds, decent meals, proper attire, or care—his father's promises have vanished into oblivion. Now it all makes sense; Robert's surprise at his name, Clover, was an attempt to erase any filial connection.

Heartbroken, he feels a pain so deep it seems irreparable. He thinks of his living parents, nearby but estranged. His brother enjoys luxuries while he suffers at the cruel hand of fate, enduring daily abuse and torment, both mental and physical.

The mention of his medical reports in the letter nags at him too, a riddle with no one to solve it. *What have I done wrong? What is Androgen Insensitivity Syndrome? Will I forever be abnormal?*

He mutters into the void until exhaustion blankets his thoughts, pulling him into a restless sleep.

Twelve

THE GREAT MASQUERADE

Feeling utterly alone in the world, Clover desires to see his Lake Fairy, the singular entity in the vast world with whom he yearns to speak. Disregarding breakfast, his appetite lost, he is consumed by memories of his father's unmet assurances outlined in the letter, the pain in his heart threatening to spill into tears.

As he prepares for school, he realizes he does not want to see Ethan. Jealousy rears its head, and the disparity between their lives feels unjust. His father's promises—his rightful comforts denied—intensify his inner turmoil. He looks at his shoes and clothes, all inferior to what Ethan wears. The weight of unfulfilled vows and a pang of resentment grip his feet as he walks to school.

He halts abruptly, deciding on the fly that it isn't important to go to school today. He doesn't want to meet his friend, or rather, his brother, today.

He is disgusted with his parents and his life. He walks through the streets of Nelson, the city he was born in—an integral part of him—yet he wishes it weren't. He wishes he were a Verdi, not a Nelson.

He strides swiftly under muted skies, neither sunny nor rainy. Clover hastens toward the lake but fears his fairy friend may not appear. She only comes when it rains or snows, and today is neither.

Upon reaching the shore, he calls out her name, but there is no response. Seated on a stone, he calls her name again, his eyes fixed on the lake's surface, hoping for ripples heralding her arrival. But only silence abides.

He wanders into the woods, wading deeper and calling her name. Time stretches as he roams with an empty belly and a burdened heart. After what feels like an eternity, overwhelmed, he sheds tears of despair, unable to hold them back any longer.

Some footsteps reverberate in the air, an orchestra composed of leaves crunching underfoot. Clover sits against a tree, his head bowed, tears married to his eyes. His nostrils tickle with his favorite scent. His Lake Fairy is near. He can smell her from afar: incense, roses, woodland notes, and a blend of herbs, growing stronger with each moment.

He rises and looks around. A voice calls out to him.

"Clover."

He turns and sees his fairy friend behind him. Overcome with emotion, he clings to her legs and cries fervently, gathering all the things he wants to tell her in his head, trying to remember the right order.

The Lake Fairy feels a pang of sorrow as she watches Clover cry. "Who hurt you, dear Clover?" she asks.

Clover breathes deeply and swallows his snot. His eyes reveal the painful truth, but he struggles to find the words. "Everyone."

She kneels and cradles his face in her hands. "Please, explain, my dear."

He wipes his tears and straightens up. "I'm not an orphan, Lake Fairy."

The Lake Fairy falls silent, gazing into his troubled eyes. "Go on."

"My parents are alive, not dead. They're here, in Nelson. But they left me. I don't know why."

The Lake Fairy straightens her back and stares into the distance. "How do you know this?"

"I found a letter in Ms. Preen's cabinet. My dad wrote it. His name is Robert Verdi. He is rich—very rich—but he did not want me." Clover bursts into tears again.

The Lake Fairy wraps her arms around him in a comforting hug and kisses his head. "My dear, I'm so sorry you've gone through this."

Words fail Clover as a lump forms in his throat, preventing him from speaking coherently. "I—my friend at—at school," he stammers, "he is my... brother, I... his—his h—house..."

The fairy listens intently, then wipes his eyes with her long black sleeves and rubs his back. "Your friend at school is actually your brother. You went to his house—is that correct?"

Clover nods. "And—and they know I live nearby, the same place they left me. But they never bothered to visit. Never, ever. They love Ethan, their son. I don't know... I don't know what I—I did wrong. There was something mentioned in the letter. Andro-insensitive... something. What is that?"

The Lake Fairy's mouth forms a thin line, and she looks away.

"Please, Lake Fairy, help—help me understand. Why me?"

The Lake Fairy watches Clover ask questions she cannot answer. She tilts her head slightly, and he notices a globule escape her eye. Silent, she furrows her brow, staring off into the distance.

"Help me, Lake Fairy," Clover pleads. "I don't want to go to school and see Ethan ever again. I don't like that he has everything—parents, a nice house, food, clothes, toys, and so many other things. But why don't I get to have any of that? What can I do to get what's mine?"

The fairy rises to her feet, her chest heaving up and down in rapid breaths. "Now you understand why I told you that you live in misery," she says. "But fate must favor you now. Enough of the games your parents played. It's time for the great masquerade."

Clover swallows hard. "Sorry?"

The Lake Fairy turns to him. "Do you want to have what's yours?"

Clover falls silent, contemplating. *Can I?* "Yes," he says, excited but apprehensive, wondering if his fairy friend truly has a solution.

"Do you want to live where you rightfully belong?" the fairy asks in an enchanting voice.

"Yes, yes." Clover nods eagerly. "Tell me how. How, Lake Fairy?"

The Lake Fairy perches on a log, legs crossed, hands resting on her knees, speaking with confidence. "For that to happen, you must do something bad."

"What bad thing?" Clover asks, his toes twitching and goosebumps rising on his skin.

"You must swap with Ethan," the fairy says. "Bring him to me and take his place."

Clover blinks in a fog of bewilderment. "How is this possible? How can I take Ethan's place? His parents would know it's me."

The fairy forms an evil smirk, and for the first time, Clover starts to believe she might be a witch. He knows she has magical powers, but the extent of her abilities remains a mystery.

"I must tell you, Clover. I'll do anything for you. You're a good child, and you deserve all the happiness in the world. There is nothing I wouldn't do to place you in your rightful place, and that, my boy, is the Verdi Mansion."

Clover watches her in awe, his mouth agape, eager to know what she plans to do and how.

"Ethan and you cannot live under the same roof. It is what it is. You must bring him to me and take his place."

"But how—"

"His parents," she pauses, then continues, "your parents won't know it's you. I'll give you an enchanted powder that will bewitch their minds. Whosoever's spirit it touches, you'll look like one." She stands and walks into the woods. "Should it touch Ethan, they'll see you as him. But you will always be Clover, even if others see you as Ethan."

Can this really happen? Clover wonders. It seems unattainable, but maybe not for his fairy friend. She has mentioned being a witch before, and this seems like one of her sorcery enactments. *Who am I to judge?*

But he thinks of Ethan. "What will you do with Ethan, Lake Fairy?" he asks, awaiting a serious answer.

The fairy gives a sardonic grin. "I'll take him to my house," she says.

Clover shivers in shock, feeling as if his heart has stopped beating. "Under the lake?" he asks, horror growing.

The fairy doesn't answer, only smiles. "Perhaps you have forgotten, dear. I'm a witch. I'm a fairy for you, but not for everyone else."

Clover feels torn. As much as he desires to take Ethan's place, he cannot endanger him. Swapping places means Ethan will live with the fairy forever, underwater. He might even cease to exist, as humans cannot breathe underwater. The fairy has magic, but Ethan does not.

He quivers at the thought. "If you take Ethan with you, will he... die?"

The fairy shakes her head. "I won't let him die. But he can never return to his house. He'll live with me, away from his parents, away from you."

Clover drops to his knees. "I can't do it," he whispers.

"What's that, dear?"

He shakes his head. "I cannot betray Ethan. It's not his fault. My parents are to blame. Why should he suffer?"

"Agreed," the fairy says. "You decide, Clover. What do you want? The same miserable life, or a chance to be where you should be—a life of luxury or a life of suffering. You choose."

Caught in a quandary, Clover is torn again—this time between his morals and the temptation of his rightful place. He thinks and rethinks as time slips away. The Lake Fairy waits patiently, singing softly as she strolls through the woods.

Clover stands rooted, unable to decide. He wants to live in Verdi Mansion. Everything belongs to him by right. He is the elder son, born before Ethan, making him the rightful heir to the Verdi family, not Ethan. He recalls stories where the second son is always seen as the "spare."

Ethan will be fine, Clover reassures himself. He will live with the Lake Fairy. Don't worry about him too much. Just go to Verdi Mansion. It's your home. You belong there.

"Have you decided, dear?" The fairy walks back toward him. "What do you want?"

Clover stirs from his spot, heaves a long sigh, and drops to the ground again. "I want Ethan's life," he says.

The fairy smiles. "Bring him to me."

Clover looks up at her, hands clasped together. "Nothing should happen to Ethan."

The fairy gives a twisted smile. "I avow nothing will happen to him," she says. "Go and bring your brother to me."

Clover stands up, turns around, and runs as fast as he can. The bag bounces on his shoulder, and each step seems to barely touch the earth. The fuel is his desire—his fervent desire to reclaim his life. He has been given a chance and doesn't want to miss it.

Once cloaked by clouds, the sky clears, revealing patches of blue, with golden rays illuminating the surroundings. Sunbeams pierce through the clouds, spotlighting Clover's ephemeral silhouette as he races through the market, heading toward his school.

His feet pound against the cobblestones, shops blur past him, and although his eyes are watery, he remains focused on his goal: to bring Ethan to his fairy friend, who will handle the rest.

As the school comes into view and Ethan remains inside the classroom, Clover anxiously waits for recess. His tension mounts with each second, knowing Ethan could emerge at any moment. Finally, the bell rings, unleashing a wave of children onto the school grounds.

Among them is Ethan, looking solitary and sad, clearly missing his best friend. Suddenly, he spots Clover by the gate, frantically waving as he rushes toward him.

Ethan stops near Clover. "Where were you? Why didn't you come to school today?"

Clover can't deny his happiness at seeing his friend, but he remembers that he is not just talking to his friend; he is speaking to his brother. It's time to take him away to the lake.

"I was—was, umm, forget it. Come with me. I need to show you something."

Ethan looks confused. "It's recess. We can't go anywhere now."

"Look, Ethan." Clover leans in, whispering close to his ear. "I met a fairy by the lake, and I want you to meet her too."

Ethan's mouth drops open. "A fairy?" He moves his lips, but no sound comes out.

"Yeah. Near the lake," Clover insists.

Clover has planted the seed of curiosity in Ethan, and now he waits.

Ethan scans the area. "Mr. Manson won't be here until the end of the school day, so I have time. But Ms. Clarkson will notice. Are you sure you saw a fairy?"

Clover nods.

Ethan stands in silence, deep in thought. Finally, he says, "Wait here."

He goes inside and returns shortly with his school bag.

I think he is ready. Good job, Clover, he thinks, smirking.

Ethan approaches him. "I told Ms. Clarkson my parents were here to pick me up."

"Didn't she ask why?" Clover asks, guiding Ethan outside the school gate.

"Yes." Ethan hurries along. "I told her my dad needed to take me to a doctor. I was sick last night. She said okay."

Clover feels a swell of pride at having convinced Ethan so quickly. They are now on their way to the lake, to the fairy.

"So, tell me, how did you meet this fairy?" Ethan asks, eager and full of questions.

Clover falls silent, unsure of what to say. "I can only show you," he repeats.

Ethan remains undeterred and excited to meet the fairy. He doesn't mind skipping school for it, believing Clover must have a good reason. Maybe this fairy is worth meeting. He walks faster, nearly running.

"Can we return by the end of the school day?" he asks Clover. "I don't want Mr. Manson to look for me and complain to my dad."

"Yes," Clover says, now leading him onto a secluded path through the dense woods. The bustling crowds fall away, replaced by serene solitude and cloudy skies beneath the green canopy.

They move further in. The sound of the lake grows louder. They draw near the shore. Clover grips Ethan's hand tightly. "Stay close to me."

Ethan fidgets, scanning for any sign of some ethereal entity. "Where is the fairy?"

Just then, a woman comes into sight, draped in night's hue, winding through the woods toward the lake where the boys stand.

Ethan gasps, his breath catching in disbelief. "Do fairies wear black clothes?" he murmurs, noticing her dark attire and tresses. "Is she a real fairy? Why is she dressed like that?"

"Don't worry. She is lovely," Clover reassures him, aware that Ethan should be concerned. The Lake Fairy will take him to her realm, giving Clover a chance to claim his place in Verdi Mansion. Though thrilling, he feels a weight of dread at seeing the excitement on Ethan's face.

"Can she do magic?" Ethan asks.

"Of course she can," Clover replies. "That's why I brought you here."

The Lake Fairy stands before the boys, smiling at Clover. "How are you, my dear?"

Clover smiles back. "I'm fine, Lake Fairy. Thank you." He tugs at

Ethan's arms. "I brought Ethan to meet you." His insides abhor him for saying that, but Clover wants what he wants.

"Hello, Miss," Ethan bows. "Are you, umm, a fairy? A real one?"

The Lake Fairy chuckles, fluttering her eyelashes slowly. "Of course, dear."

She holds out a jute bag and places it on Ethan's head. Then she mutters something with her eyes closed and hands the bag to Clover.

"You're clear, honey." She spins around, tossing her hands in the air. "Go forth where fortune heads strong. Accept not misery but where you belong."

She whirls back to Clover. "You'll be protected if you keep this bag. Remember, never throw it in the trash. If this powder slips from your hand, everything could revert to what you do not want. Stay true to the path and where your fate resides. Let not the magic of masquerade scatter or hide. You two of the same origin cannot dwell in one space, but I pledge to care for him and ensure his life is safe. Yours, Clover, awaits elsewhere, so go and find it. Take this bag with you to let the spell bind."

Ethan stands befuddled, listening to the fairy's riddles, unsure why she placed the bag on his head and then handed it to Clover. His eyes grow heavy; his limbs weaken, for he remains clueless about what's happening. He wants to ask the fairy to perform some magic tricks, but it seems her enchantments are already coursing through him.

The spell hits him, slowly relaxing him, one organ at a time. Clover watches Ethan blink, holding on to him to prevent his fall.

Meanwhile, the spell toys with Ethan's senses—a dizzying maelstrom. His world spins, and the lake and emerald forest fade into a kaleidoscope of bewildering colors. With each breath, the enchantment wraps tighter, weakening his core until, with a stumble, he collapses, Clover unable to bear his weight.

The fairy looks accomplished, releasing a breath of achievement. She steps closer and hoists Ethan's body, gently touching his cheeks. He appears to be in a deep sleep. Clover stands shocked, his heart plunging at the thought of losing his friend—his brother.

"Is he okay?" he asks, his voice trembling.

"He's fine, just unconscious," the fairy answers placidly. "It's easier for me to take him this way. He won't resist."

Ethan's head rests in the fairy's arms as she begins to sing a soothing lullaby to his disarrayed soul. Clover clutches the enchanted bag tightly.

"That bag," the fairy says, turning to him. "Keep it with you. Always. You'll be known as Ethan Verdi from this moment on. Go and take your rightful place. Never come back here again."

Clover's legs wobble. "Can I not come to see you?"

"Clover has ceased to exist," the fairy says.

"But—but—"

"Don't think too much, Clover. Go on and never return to me. If you do, it will destroy everything."

With Ethan in her arms, the fairy moves toward the enchanted woods, her sweet murmurs filling the air. Ethan remains in her care, his body swaying as she walks over the rocks.

Clover's heart sinks. He stands frozen, wanting to see if Ethan is taken into the lake, to see if he will survive beneath the water.

"Go, Clover!" The fairy's voice echoes. "Do not linger here."

Clover shivers and whirls around, picking up Ethan's school bag from the ground. He runs toward the new identity his fairy friend has given him—something that will change his life entirely. He assures himself that Ethan will be fine and that the Lake Fairy will take care of him.

But haunting thoughts continue to invade his mind. Soon he reaches the school and sees children streaming onto the grounds. Everyone is leaving, but Clover doesn't know where to go or what to do, so he stands at the gate, unsure, his body trembling with fear, his throat parched.

Ethan's car rolls by and stops at the gate where Clover stands. Mr. Manson steps out. Clover remains rooted to the spot, awkwardly looking at Mr. Manson as he approaches.

"Let's go home, sir," Mr. Manson says, taking Clover's school bag. "Why are you standing here?"

Clover is stunned. Did the magic work? Does Mr. Manson believe I am Ethan? He glances at the jute bag in his hands, his dream life enchanted by this powder.

Clover, now Ethan in disguise, clutches the enchanted bag and shoves it into his pocket, stepping into the life he's fashioned. This time, seated in the car without his faithful friend, he feels joy, knowing he won't face the scorn he endured before.

He savors the journey, bidding the orphanage farewell with a fleeting glance, determined never to look back. Gone is Clover; he has relinquished that name forever. Now he is Ethan—a Verdi—journeying to the rightful place where his destiny lies.

The car veers right, entering a neighborhood of posh homes. Approaching his residence, where he was born, albeit not raised, he prepares to reclaim what's his.

The car stops, and Mr. Manson opens the door for him. He smiles, relishing the treatment he receives. Entering the grand mansion, he vows to explore every nook, revel in each toy, and run through the corridors. His heart flutters. *Will everyone here also recognize me as Ethan?*

He feels nervous as he walks down the foyer but stops when he sees Robert Verdi seated at the dining table, a newspaper in his hand, sipping tea.

Robert senses his presence, turning to him, his eyes hidden behind reading glasses. "You?"

Clover freezes. The tone of *you* feels unpaternal. He fears Robert suspects him, but he isn't sure. His heart pounds aggressively, racing like a sprinter, while his surroundings blur. He hears footsteps approaching, feeling the cold touch of the floor beneath him.

Thirteen

GIRLY BOY

"Ethan, my boy," Robert cries, horrified. "Do something, doctor. What happened to my son?"

Robert sits beside the hospital bed, looking at his son, Clover, disguised as Ethan.

"Ethan, my baby," Samantha sobs, caressing Clover's head.

"Mr. and Mrs. Verdi, please let me assess him," the doctor says.

He places his stethoscope on Clover's chest. Then, feeling for a pulse on his wrist, he adds, "He is fine, Mr. Verdi."

"Then why did he faint?" Robert asks. "And why isn't he getting up?"

"Ethan had a panic attack," the doctor explains. "However, it is strange. Very uncommon for boys his age."

"A panic attack?" Robert looks bewildered. "He's never—I mean, what for?"

The doctor purses his lips. "I cannot say. Is he afraid of anything? Does he have any phobias?"

Robert's head shakes with incredulity. "Nothing that I know of."

"I see. Once he's awake, you may take him home and make sure he eats well," the doctor says, placing the stethoscope around his neck.

Clover is awake now, though he keeps his eyes closed. He can hear the doctor talking to his parents, who seem extremely worried for him, and he enjoys the feeling, wanting to savor it a little longer. What harm can it do?

Although he doesn't know why he fainted. He's only fainted once, and that was because of a spider in his room. *Why was I so terrified of seeing Robert Verdi? Was it his tone?* One thing Clover knows for sure is that they both believe he is Ethan. He smiles softly but also wants to go home, to where he truly belongs—the Verdi Mansion.

The doctor departs. Robert and Samantha return to his bedside. Clover hears Samantha sniffling and feels pity.

Meanwhile, Robert's breaths grow louder. "What are you crying for now? You've done what you wanted, woman. Neglected my son like he was an object. Look what you've done to him."

"I didn't do anything," Samantha's words waver, choked by sorrow.

"You're right, Samantha. You didn't do anything. This wouldn't have happened if you had been a proper mother to my son. Shame on you."

Robert turns to Clover, caressing his cheeks. "My boy. I'm sorry."

Clover hears Robert sniffling. He looks at Samantha with a grave expression. "What if I arrange for him a proper mother?"

Samantha's eyes flood with horror, knowing what Robert means. "It's not like I don't care for him. I've been sick, you know that, for ages."

"I don't care." Robert shakes his head. "You may go live with your filthy sister. I couldn't care less. I'm done with you. Done with your illness."

"I had a hysterectomy, Robert." Samantha takes a sharp breath. "I'm on hormone therapy."

"And that's exactly why I'm done with you," Robert says, gritting his teeth. "Your womb is done; you can't bear me more children. I wished for many children, but you"—he rises, stepping closer, his breath ruffling her hair—"just gave me one heir, not to mention the anomaly you popped years ago, whom we had to get rid of."

Anomaly? What does it mean? Clover thinks, his heart racing, his chest rising and falling. He tries to control it but can't help it.

"You have no heart, Robert." Samantha scrambles to her feet. "You refer to our son as filth, anomaly, and whatnot. Aren't you ashamed? Aren't you sorry that you're the only one responsible for my situation? You gave me wounds, Robert, that collapsed my womb. You're no man."

Robert turns away, flaring his nostrils, then pivots on his heels, his fists clenched. Freeing his fists, and with a flick of a hand, his sharp percussion strikes her cheek. It hits so hard it stings and burns.

"Sit down and stay quiet," he commands.

Clover trembles, hearing the slap echo through the air like a discordant note, but his eyes remain closed. He knows what has happened and is afraid to see the sight.

Samantha doesn't cry, though she presses her cheeks, unable to soothe her florid skin. "That's all you can do. Beat me. Ignore me." She sits beside Clover again.

"Because you deserve it," Robert retorts. "Should my son feel neglected again by you, your exit from my house is inevitable. Do you understand?"

"Of course," Samantha mutters. "So you can bring your mistress to Verdi Mansion."

"What did you say?" Robert's head tilts, eyes narrowing.

But Clover heard it, even if he didn't understand. One thing he knows is that his parents do not get along. His father never liked Nathan and left him at Whispering Hearts. His mother, however, seems to have been suffering, but the reason is uncharted. Could it be because of me?

He wants to know the truth behind his abandonment. Why is my father so bitter? Why is my mother so helpless? He wants to know it all.

Clover slowly opens his eyes, but Robert catches him. "Ethan!" He holds him tight with trembling arms, thrilled his once-shuttered eyes have opened. "My Ethan," he whispers, kissing his cheeks.

Samantha caresses Clover's hair. "How are you, my dear? What happened?" Her voice chokes.

Robert keeps him close to his chest, refusing to let him go. Samantha wants to hug him too, but Robert doesn't allow it, angry at her for failing as a mother.

Clover looks at Samantha's thwacked cheeks and feels sorry for her, but he can't say anything until he learns the truth. For now, he enjoys being in his father's arms, his fingers brushing against the enchanted bag the fairy gave him, safely tucked in his pocket.

Robert pulls away from Clover and notices his shabby clothes, which aren't Ethan's. They belong to Clover.

"These clothes," he says. "Where did you get them?"

"Yeah," Samantha adds. "Look at the shirt's inseams. Whose clothes are you wearing?"

Clover gulps. *Why didn't I think of that?* He should have worn Ethan's clothing or something nicer to enter Verdi Mansion.

"My ... I—" He stops. *Do I sound like Clover or Ethan?* He glances at both of them, who look confused. He starts again. "I spoiled them while playing. Umm, my friend Clover gave me his clothes."

"That's why they look, er, strange," Samantha says. "How did you spoil your clothes?"

"Oh, please, Sam." Robert sighs. "They are just clothes. If they're soiled, they're soiled. I hope he tossed them. Did you, son?"

"Y—yes, I did," Clover replies, exhaling deeply.

Suddenly, Robert's face turns grim. "Your friend, Clover," he says, "how's he doing?"

Clover holds his breath. "He is fine," he says. "He's gone."

And Clover has indeed disappeared, contemplating his own vanishing act, crafting a story for his parents and Ethan's parents. Faced with inevitable questions, he concocts a narrative, half true, half false.

"Gone where?" Samantha interrupts, equally curious.

Clover realizes his story must be convincing enough so Ethan's parents won't ask about him anymore. "He left the city today," he says, avoiding eye contact. "He moved to another city with his parents."

"Where?" Samantha asks.

"I don't know. I—I didn't quite catch the name," Clover replies.

"Good," Robert mutters. "Now, we must stop talking about him and ask you an important question."

Clover looks at him nervously. "Yes?"

"How did you faint?" Robert asks. "Did you get scared?"

"I saw—saw a ... spider." Clover fashions a fib.

"And you fainted?" Samantha asks. "Are you afraid of spiders?"

"Odd that you two don't know," the doctor says, returning to his ward. "I asked you if he had any phobias."

"Honestly, doctor, we didn't ... know," Robert says, flashing a nervous grin.

"Me neither," Samantha adds, resting her palm on her right cheek.

"Hmm." The doctor leans over to check on Clover again. "I think he is good to go."

"Great, thanks." Robert shakes hands with the doctor. "Come on, son. Let's go home."

Clover and his parents head back to Verdi Mansion. Once they arrive, everyone gathers in Ethan's room.

"Have some rest, my boy." Robert pulls the covers up over Clover once he settles into bed. "Your mother will get you something to eat, all right?"

"Hot chocolate," he says suddenly.

How can he forget his treasured libation of all? Under Agatha's guardianship, it remains out of reach until the holidays, and he's eager to savor it without the wait or the fear that all the marshmallows will be gone by the time it's his turn. He is convinced he can have it—and that, too, multiple times a day—during brisk morns or sun-kissed afternoons, amid the rain or snow, and every day. As long as he is Ethan, he can have whatever he wants.

"For sure, my baby," Samantha says. "What else do you want to eat?"

"Just get him his favorite," Robert says, his barbed tongue casting its bitter sting. "If you know what it is."

"Okay." Samantha smiles nervously, then looks at Robert. "I'll go get some—something."

Robert sits next to Clover. "Would you like me to read you a story?" he asks, reaching for a book from the chest beside the bed.

"Later," Clover says. "I want to have hot chocolate first."

"Of course, my son. Your mother should be bringing it soon."

"Don't worry about your mother, my dear," Imelda says, manifesting in the room unexpectedly.

Clover's sight darts to her, startled by her sudden arrival. She's the same woman who served them lunch the day before. She places a polished brown tray on the table, setting down a mug of steaming hot chocolate, croissants, and sandwiches. Clover's mouth waters.

He wonders how Imelda brought his favorite things so quickly. Samantha must have left only moments ago—there's no way she could have reached the kitchen and delegated the task so fast.

"Thanks," Clover says.

As he drinks his hot chocolate and bites into the sandwiches, he notices Imelda's crude gaze on Robert—a stare that makes Clover uncomfortable. However, Robert seems to enjoy it, looking at her intently, far from the way he meets his wife's eyes.

Clover observes the gestures they share: Imelda biting her lip and toying with her skirt, behaving differently than before. He's old enough to sense that it's not right. Robert looks at her from head to toe, leering with scrutiny.

Feeling the need to interrupt, Clover says, "Can you get me some hash browns?"

Imelda breaks her connection with Robert and redirects her attention to Clover. "Finish what's on your plate, my dear. I'll bring you hash browns shortly."

She turns her gaze back to Robert, slowly approaching him.

Clover feels a surge of anger and disgust. "Bring me some now!" he commands, surprised by his own confidence and tone. "I don't want these krosont." He pushes the plate away and pulls at his father's arm.

Imelda's composure falters at Clover's interruption, irritation entering her demeanor. "Finish what's on your plate," she repeats, this time tersely, clearly annoyed by the disruption.

Robert's expression shifts. "He told you he doesn't want it, so get him what he wants," he says firmly. "Don't say no to my son."

"Sure, sir," she says with a stiff smile. "I'll bring hash browns right now." Pursing her lips, she exits the room.

Clover shakes his head, wondering if Ethan knows Imelda's intentions. Then his stomach sinks at the thought of him—Ethan. Where would he be? What is he doing now? Is he comfortable?

Sure, he is. Lake Fairy is with him. Clover reassures himself not to feel guilty.

"Dad?" Clover turns to Robert.

"Hmm." Robert smiles at him. "What is it, Ethan?"

Clover hesitates, pushing the tray, still full of delectable fare, aside. "Am I—I your, umm, only child?"

Robert narrows his eyes. "Of course you are. Who else do you see in this house?"

A forced smile tugs at the corners of Clover's mouth. Disheartened by the realization that Nathan means nothing to Robert, he loses interest in discussing his former self. "Okay," he mutters.

Yet for Clover, understanding the reason behind his abandonment is critical. Consequently, he begins to shadow Robert closely.

As days morph into a strategic game of proximity, Clover, masquerading as Ethan, embeds himself in Robert's world. He skips school, feigns illness (though not severely enough to avoid dawdling in Robert's office), and silently observes his dealings and movements, even accompanying him on outings with partners and employees.

Referred to as Verdi Jr., he takes pride in the title, while Robert, too, is pleased with his heir in the making.

Throughout this time, Clover has tried to seek the truth about his own identity from Robert. On one occasion, he asked, "Would you want another son, Dad?"

To which Robert replied, "I already have you, my boy."

It seems futile to ask him more about Clover. Robert wouldn't budge, so Clover decides to wait for the right moment.

Samantha insists that Ethan return to school after being off for almost three days, but Robert enjoys his son's company and tells Samantha he will resume school the following week. Clover needs considerable time to adjust to being Ethan. School will overwhelm him. Besides, everyone will ask about Clover, and he'll struggle to handle it.

One day, sitting in his room, Clover thinks about Whispering Hearts. *Ms. Preen may be looking for me,* he wonders. He has been missing for the last three days. There will be posters everywhere about his disappearance, making him think that if his parents discover Clover's absence, they will learn he has lied about himself. They will know he is the same Clover, the undesirable boy they abandoned years ago. *I must leave Nelson,* he decides, and heads straight to Robert's office to sort things out.

Sitting in a chair across from him, he says, "Can I ask you something?"

Robert, busy with some files, doesn't mind the interruption. He turns to Clover. "Of course."

Clover knows Robert is the only one who can help him fulfill his plan. So, he makes a request that he knows Robert cannot deny. "I don't like my school, Dad."

Robert leans forward, his brows raised. "Why don't you like your school?"

Clover stares at the floor. "Umm, just like that," he says. "I was thinking if, you know, we could move back to Kamloops." He presses his lips together and looks at him shyly, hoping he will approve of the idea and allow him to leave Nelson for good. The Lake Fairy has already asked him never to return to the lake—to her. He wants to avoid school and the reality of Clover's disappearance.

Robert leans back in his chair, scratching his head. "Why don't you like living here? I thought you were happy."

Clover shakes his head. "No, I'm not." Then he considers that if he tells him he doesn't want to study with less affluent students at a public school and prefers to be around wealthy children like himself, maybe his father will agree. "My classmates are strange. I have to share my meals with them. They don't even bring their own. The school is way too old and smelly." He sticks out his tongue. "Yuck!"

Robert sneers in a muted way, proud that his son is becoming like him. "I'll see, my boy. It hasn't even been two months." He leans back in his chair. "Samantha wanted to come here. She won't agree."

"Well, then, make her agree," Clover insists. "You can, I know. Why doesn't Mom want to leave Nelson?" Though he knows the answer, he ensures it doesn't show.

Robert sighs. "She's got some old wounds that she enjoys suffering from. She never wants to get over them, that woman." He sighs again, this time more deeply. "I'll talk to her." He leans back in his chair, steepling his hands and biting his lip. "Maybe we can... bring Imelda with us, leaving Samantha here until she feels better about traveling."

Clover begins to breathe rapidly. *Of course*, he thinks, knowing why Imelda is preferred over Samantha. "No," he says crossly.

Robert narrows his eyes and leans forward. "But why? Imelda takes good care of you."

Clover remains tense, holding his gaze. "Imelda will not go with us. Sack her or whatever. Mom will go with us. She is my mother, not Imelda."

Robert finds this odd, suspecting his son may have caught wind of his relationship with Imelda. As Ethan matures, Robert feels obligated to maintain his image as a good father and husband. "Whatever you say, my son. Samantha, not Imelda, will be going to Kamloops with us."

With an exuberant fist pump, Clover celebrates. "Thanks, Dad."

The dream of moving from his birthplace to Ethan's birthplace captivates his mind. Though he feels sad to leave a city that gave him his name, he is no longer attached to Nelson. Besides, he can never visit his fairy friend again. He doesn't want to pass by the orphanage where he was raised every day on his way to school. It's better to leave it all behind and rebuild his life.

There is a shattering sound of glass, startling both of them as they turn toward the doorway. Imelda stands frozen in place, a tray in her hands but no glasses. The broken shards lie scattered on the floor. A grimace crosses her face.

Robert quickly rises and rushes to her side. "What happened, Imelda?"

Clover hears Imelda snorting and Robert conversing with her in whispers. His cheeks bloom, a twisted smile on his face. *She deserves it,* he thinks.

Clover flicks a glance toward the doorway and sees Robert holding Imelda's hands, which troubles him. Imelda shakes her head vigorously, clearly in discord. A frown tugs at Clover's lips; he disapproves of Robert's consoling gesture and believes Imelda deserves a reprimand for breaking the expensive glasses.

Resolute, he strides over, interrupting their moment. Robert quickly withdraws his hands from Imelda's. Standing beside Robert, Clover's eyes convey his dissenting stance. "Clean up the mess," he tells Imelda.

Imelda narrows her eyes. "Sorry? What did you say?"

"Clean it up," Clover insists. "You made a mess, so you clean it. Right, Dad?" He looks at Robert for support.

Robert forces a smile. "Y—yes," he says, though his lips barely move.

Imelda refuses to comply. "I won't," she shouts, her sobs booming as she flees, her voice ringing through the vast mansion as she yells, "I hate you. I hate you both."

Robert looks uncomfortable, but Clover feels a surge of satisfaction at the outcome. Crossing his arms, he tells Robert, "I'm heading to my room to start packing."

Imelda's outbursts still resonate in the hall. Robert keeps looking in the direction she fled, his heart stalling, yet he cannot let it show, especially in front of Clover. He nods in approval to Clover, who then strides toward his room.

Ethan's closet is filled with clothes. Clover stands before it, contemplating what to pack for Kamloops. He decides to remove some shirts, pants, and toys, spreading them on the bed but unable to find a suitcase or bag to put them in. At least he can arrange them neatly, so he begins folding his clothes. Having folded his own clothes for a while, he knows how to do it.

Eventually, he grows tired and lies on the bed with his eyes closed, but all he sees behind his eyelids are posters and news about Clover's disappearance, which makes him anxious. He doesn't want his parents to find out about him. What if they discover he's taken Ethan's place and throw him out again?

Breathing heavily, he snaps his eyes open, wiping the beads of sweat from his upper lip, thinking, *How can I make things right?*

It has been three days, and Agatha would have done something by now. Clover knows she is afraid of the authorities, so she may keep it low, but what if she doesn't?

Then, an idea strikes him. He reaches for a pen and paper and begins to write a letter to Agatha as Clover. In it, he explains that he has moved to another city, hoping this will convince her that she no longer needs to worry about him.

He could post the letter, but there is a faster way: Mr. Manson. He can ask him to drop off the letter at the orphanage. He will do it for him—for Ethan—in a heartbeat.

After finishing the letter, he sprints downstairs and outside to the driveway, where Mr. Manson is cleaning the car. No wonder it always shines like silk.

"Mr. Manson," Clover calls out as he approaches. "Could you please drop this letter at Whispering Hearts?"

Mr. Manson takes the letter but appears surprised. "That orphanage?"

"Yeah." Clover tries to sound confident, already prepared for the next question. "Clover gave this letter to me, er, to give to his friend at the orphanage," he explains.

"The boy who came here last week?" Mr. Manson asks, his lips forming a distorted line. "Where is he?"

Clover straightens, trying to project confidence. "He's left the city."

Mr. Manson shrugs. "All right. I'll drop it off this afternoon."

"Thanks." Clover beams, feeling relieved that his problem is resolved.

As he reenters the mansion, he stops near the dining table and notices a newspaper. He flips it over, praying there is no news about him. Luckily, he does not find any mention of missing Clover in the paper.

Putting the newspaper back, he walks up the stairs to his room, hoping his letter achieves what he intends.

"Ethan, stop," Samantha calls from behind him.

Clover halts and waits for her to catch up. "Mom?"

Samantha reaches him at the last step, a smile on her face that he has never seen before. "How are you, Ethan?" she asks.

A jittery smile is all Clover can manage. "Good," he says.

Samantha's attempt to speak begins with a hesitant parting of her lips, but then an uncertainty interrupts her, causing a pause as her mouth hesitates mid-action. She reconsiders, her lips closing briefly in a subtle press as she struggles with a change of heart once again. Moments pass, and then she makes another attempt, opening her mouth again.

"I want—wanted, umm, I would like to … spend some time with you," she says. "In your room, if you don't mind."

Clover nods. "Of course, Mom." He takes her hand and leads her to his room.

As Samantha enters Ethan's room, she notices the pile of clothes and toys on his bed but doesn't seem surprised. Clover keeps glancing at her, catching her smile from time to time.

"Since when have you become a big boy?" She turns to Clover and pinches his cheeks, making them turn red. "Taking care of your stuff like a big boy."

"We are leaving, Mom," Clover says, glancing at her sideways. "I don't know if Dad told you."

Samantha nods. "I know. Robert just told me," she says, then looks at Clover. "He also mentioned that you don't want to live in Nelson anymore and want to attend a private school." She lowers her head. "I get it. I understand." Sighing, she turns to him. "I'll help you pack."

Clover is relieved that Samantha doesn't disapprove. Now, they can become a family like no other, away from people like Imelda, far from Nelson, where haunting childhood memories cannot reach him. He sits on the leather settee, which is too large for his small frame. "Can I tell you something?"

"Sure," Samantha says, sifting through Ethan's clothes.

Clover pauses, contemplating how to articulate his thoughts. After a moment, he speaks. "I heard you and Dad ... that day."

Samantha spins around, her eyes widening. "Sorry?"

"I heard you and Dad talking about ... your son the other day."

Samantha walks toward Clover and kneels beside him. "You're our son."

Clover sees a nervous grin on her face. "No. I meant the other son."

Disbelief flashes across Samantha's face as she struggles to comprehend how Ethan discovered her other son. *Was he pretending to sleep all along?* she wonders. *What else has he heard?* Swallowing hard, she looks away and says, "We don't have another child."

Really? Clover thinks.

Yet Samantha's heart tells a different story. Emotions clash within her like waves against a cliff. She utters lies without shame, filled with guilt, regret, and helplessness as she recalls her firstborn, a forgotten chapter in her life.

"I know, Mom." Clover stands up from the settee. "I heard it. Don't lie to me. You and Dad were talking about my brother. I wasn't sleeping."

Samantha freezes, her eyes widening like a deer caught in headlights. Each word from Clover dismantles the façade she has constructed. Her hands tremble, and words falter on her lips. Yet she knows she must respond; it will alleviate her burden.

"Yes," she finally admits, staring blankly at the floor.

"Sorry?" Clover cannot hear her. "Did I have a brother?"

Samantha is afraid to meet his gaze. For her, it's Ethan who stands by her side. She wraps her arms around herself and sits on the floor, shutting her eyes. "Yes—yes, you have a brother, but I don't know where he is."

It angers Clover to his core. "You don't know where your son is?" he demands.

Samantha slowly lifts her head. "We left him at an orphanage," she confesses, holding her breath.

"Which orphanage?" Clover asks, though he already knows the answer.

Samantha is caught in a momentary lapse, shocked by his mention of the word *orphanage*. "How do you know what an orphanage is?" she asks.

Clover breathes rapidly. "I know a lot of things."

"You do?" Samantha takes a deep breath, the mere mention of this word sending chills down her spine and triggering a flood of memories. "Whispering Hearts," she mutters, recalling the haunting day. "The orphanage is called Whispering Hearts."

She has now confirmed Clover's conjectures. His lips begin to jut out, but he strives to remain composed. "Why—why did you leave your son?"

Samantha feels her heart tighten. The weight of the truth presses down on her, inducing pain as it laces through her chest and into her mind. The truth is never easy, but it can be liberating.

Caught off guard by the mention of their son, her fingers interlace and tremble, her eyes narrating the untold tale she holds within. She bows her head, unsure of how to express herself. But Clover's insistence breaks through this cloak of quiet; each "why" demands the truth she hesitates to reveal.

Samantha believes Ethan is innocent, yet she is torn, tangled in the uncertainty of whether he can grasp the complexity of her reality. Her mind whirls in a pandemonium of confusion and helplessness, caught between shielding Ethan's innocence and fearing that his quest for answers might lead him astray if she remains silent.

At last, she relents, understanding that this truth can no longer be veiled. She looks him in the eye and says, "Your brother is neither a boy nor a girl."

Fourteen

UNDER THE LAKE

Clover tilts his head, puzzled by what his mother just said. "I don't understand, Mom."

Samantha clutches her cardigan tightly and stands up, stepping away from Clover. "His name is Nathan." She exhales sharply. "He was... born with a genetic condition: Androgen Insensitivity Syndrome."

Clover recalls the medical term Robert used in the letter. "So, it's a disease?" he asks.

Samantha faces the window and says, "It's a condition that makes you a... third gender."

Clover blinks owlishly. "So, is he not a"—he stops to reconsider—"boy?"

Samantha shakes her head, swallowing hard. "Genetically, he is male. But he... does not have male features. To society, he is not a boy."

"What is he then?" Clover is shocked and frazzled, remembering Rodney's remark about *girly boy.* "Male means boy, right? If he is born male, why is he not a boy?"

"He doesn't have what boys have to be boys," Samantha explains, her chest tightening. "He is stuck and torn between two genders."

Clover's brows knit together, his expression a riddle. "What do boys have to be boys?" he asks.

Samantha turns to him, her mouth agape. "How do I explain this to you? You're so... young."

"I'll understand," Clover insists.

Samantha pinches her brows and nods reluctantly. "Androgen insensitivity is a rare condition. It means..." She looks at his small face, at his saturated cheeks, and adds, "You're too young to understand all of this. We should stop this conversation."

"I want to know, please," Clover says, taking a step forward.

Samantha sighs and turns to face him. "When a typical male body does not respond to androgen, which is the male hormone, they do not develop into males. Instead, they have parts that resemble females." She glances back at Clover's confused expression.

"What parts?" Clover asks softly, his hands moving to his pants as he recalls the unusual basins he saw at school. He may already know the answer, yet stands there with his mouth slightly open. "Male parts," he whispers. "So, that's what those basins are for. I'm not allowed to use the boys' restroom because I can't. I can never. I've always squatted on the toilet seat."

Samantha looks at Clover in horror.

Clover continues, "I was kept away from other children and given a separate room. Even at school, I was told to use the staff restroom. Now I understand." He stares into the distance. "The male parts," he mutters. "I am not fit to be either."

Rodney's words echo in his ears: *What did I hit? A toe?*

"A toe," Clover says. "That's all I have."

Samantha steps closer. "What are you talking about, Ethan? I don't understand any of this. Separated from other children? Using the staff restroom? What's going on? A toe?"

"That's all I have, Mom," Clover says, looking at her. "I'm not worthy. You did the right thing." His eyes are as red as wine, but no tears fall. "I've never been worthy."

"What makes you say that?" Samantha cups his face. "You're perfect, my boy."

Clover feels a sinking feeling in his chest. "I'm not," he exclaims, walking toward the window and reaching for the enchanted bag in his pocket. "I'm not perfect," he repeats, flinging the window open as a cool breeze rushes in. Turning away from Samantha, he scatters the enchanted powder and throws the bag into the open air.

"What was that? What did you just throw out?" Samantha asks, looking toward the window.

Clover remains still, rooted to the ground. He understands the implications of his actions. The bag thrown outside signifies that his life as Ethan has also been cast away by his own hands.

Samantha approaches him, her footsteps drawing near, causing Clover's heartbeat to quicken. He is uncertain whether the spell has already lifted, but he will soon find out. Samantha places her hand on his shoulder, sending a shiver down his spine. Reluctant to face her, he stands still, holding his breath. Samantha grips both his shoulders and turns him to face her. Clover bows his head but does not resist. As he looks up, the veil of illusion fades, and the magical mask disappears.

Samantha's eyes widen in astonishment. The enchantment is broken. She sees Clover, not Ethan. Gasping, she staggers and falls to the floor. "You? How? Where is... Ethan?"

Clover's eyes are bloodshot, his lips quivering. He feels sorry for her. "I understand now," he says. "I'm sorry."

Samantha blinks rapidly, staring at him in disbelief. "What's happening? How did you appear... and where is—where is my boy?"

"I don't know, Mom," Clover says.

Samantha's ears turn red. "Mom? Why are you calling me that?"

"I'm sorry." Clover lowers his head.

Samantha rises from the floor, her head spinning. She feels faint but manages to steady herself with the footboard. "Who are you?"

Clover realizes he is gulping down saliva but soon understands that he is parched. However, asking Samantha for water doesn't feel right. Why would she bring him water after he made her lose her son while living a life of pretense under her nose, under Robert's nose? Unsure of what to do next, he drops to his knees, hands folded in a plea. "I'm so sorry," he says. Despite his efforts, tears begin to flow, and his voice chokes. "I—I didn't know the reason."

"What are you saying?" Samantha places a hand on her chest. "What are you sorry for?"

Clover wipes his eyes, his rubicund cheeks still damp. "I'm that Clover you got rid of years ago."

Samantha balks in surprise. She blinks in disbelief, then a slow smile manifests on her lips. She bends down, touches his ears, then asks, "Are you really?"

Clover nods, keeping his head lowered.

The room falls silent. Samantha's smile fades, replaced by expressions of shame and guilt that cause her to avert her gaze. With a sorrowful shake of her head, she instinctively covers her mouth, but muffled sobs escape—the audible remnants of her inner unrest that Clover perceives. She sweats profusely, trying to stifle her cries, but the emotions are overwhelming, a mix of remorse and anger.

Anchored to the floor, her back hunched, Samantha suddenly cannot contain her feelings any longer. She lets out a shrill cry.

Clover shivers.

The haunting intensity of her cries could shatter glass—loud enough to draw people into the room—and that's the last thing Clover wants. He doesn't want anyone to come in, especially Robert, so he goes to secure the door and then returns to Samantha, kneeling by her side, concerned and confused by her petrified state.

Finally, she looks up. Her wide-eyed shock reveals deep distress; it unnerves Clover. He wonders if she is accustomed to crying like this, pondering the habitual distress and emotional outbursts reflected in the perpetual, haunting shadows beneath her eyes. His heartbeat quickens, yet Samantha remains prone, immobilized by her emotions.

"Please get up," Clover begs. "Please."

Samantha pulls him into a clinch so tight it binds him in an unbreakable shackle. Her kisses dampen his forehead as tears continue to flow from her eyes. "I knew it was you," she whispers, squeezing him tighter.

Clover feels trapped despite his attempts to break free. But Samantha's hold intensifies; he feels uncomfortable yet is ensnared by her, newly basking in the warmth of maternal love that has been absent from his life for so long. Despite the flood of affection, uncertainty lingers, and Clover wonders if this outpouring of love stems from guilt or if she is trying to atone for her past mistakes.

Abruptly, Samantha pulls back and cradles Clover's face in her hands.

"Help me," she implores, her voice overlaying with plea and desperation. "Help me understand. How are you here? Please tell me—oh dear Lord—I just can't comprehend any of this. How is it that you know who I am to you?"

Clover is momentarily speechless. He looks at her distressed face. "From the letter," he finally says.

A trickle of snot runs from Samantha's nostrils due to her relentless crying, but she brushes it aside and continues, "The letter that Robert left?"

Clover nods. "Yes."

Samantha stares at the floor, recalling that day. "It's my fate, my awful fate. I couldn't do anything for you. He took your name along with Verdi." She takes a deep breath and adds, "He gave you the name Clover. Told me years later." She looks up, seeing Clover before her, quiet and resilient. "You're angry with me, with us, aren't you?"

Clover shakes his head. "Why would I be?"

"Because we left you, my baby," Samantha cries. "We are bad parents."

"To a bad child like me," Clover says quietly. "You did nothing wrong. I deserved it."

"Why do you say that?" Samantha asks.

Clover's intermittent breaths choke his throat. He prepares to speak, but words fail him. He inhales deeply and slowly. Samantha watches him intently.

"I'm a girly boy," he admits, sitting on the floor. "For years, I thought I was special. I had a separate room with no roommates. I was bullied by Rodney for many years. He always said I'm not a boy, but I thought it was because I liked pink." Clover lets out a soft snort, resembling a sob. "One day, he beat me up while making fun of me." He looks down. "I don't have anything there. A toe," he glances at Samantha, "a toe he tells me I have. I don't know what else I was supposed to have."

Samantha's lips form a silent cry. She listens without interrupting.

Clover continues, "Even at school, I was told to use the staff bathroom, not the boys'. Again, I thought I must be special, receiving special treatment from everyone, even at school. But I didn't realize they were keeping the other boys away from me. I'm not normal. I don't have what other boys have, making me worthy of nothing."

"You're worthy, my son," Samantha says, grasping his hands. "No one is worthy to have you. We failed. We all failed."

"Then why didn't you ever visit me? You were here for a month. Why didn't it ever cross your mind to come see me at the orphanage?" Clover withdraws his hands and turns away. "I read in the letter that Dad promised I would get a comfortable bed, clothes, and food. Why didn't I ever get that? Why did I get everything used—from my cracked shoes to my clothes that were either too big or too small for me? I'm two years older than Ethan but the same size as him." He begins to cry. "Tell me why. How is it that I don't grow the same way as Ethan?"

Samantha nods slowly, taking protracted breaths. "I'm s—sorry."

"He gets proper meals. I don't," Clover shouts. "So he grows while I don't. I must walk several miles, but for him, there are cars. After I walk for a long time, I get hungry again. It feels like all the food goes into my legs and nothing remains in my tummy."

Samantha comes near Clover. "Robert has been sending money to Agatha Preen for many years," she says. "She wrote to us that you were comfortable and happy with the other children. Last month, she wrote that you were transferred to a foster home. After I insisted—rather begged —Robert decided to move back to Nelson. I wanted to see you, but I didn't know where you were. Robert wouldn't tell me anything."

"I was here all the time, Mom," Clover says, his lips pressed thin.

"You knew, Robert, you knew everything," Samantha mutters, glaring past Clover. "You never received anything she claimed you did?"

"I never got anything better than anyone else," he says, shaking his head.

"That means Agatha just kept the money and never spent it on you," Samantha says, gritting her teeth. "She is one foul—" She resists the temptation, although her insides propel her to strangulate Agatha for starving her child and embezzling funds. "I'll deal with her," she whispers. "I won't let this go."

Clover seems uninterested in Samantha's avowed intent to confront Agatha, so he continues, "I had no one to talk to. I would go to Ms. Preen to ask permission to visit the market or sometimes the lake. She never said no; I thought she cared for me, but she punished me a few times for being late. But you know, Mom, I never understood when she said, *Just don't die.* It was strange that she always said that to me. Many times, she called me filth and said it was her bad luck to end up with me. I couldn't say anything at all. But now it makes sense. Of course, I deserved it."

Samantha seethes. *How dare she?* she thinks, finally realizing the harm Agatha has inflicted on her child. It is unforgivable. Her heart feels like it is on fire, her eyes burning with rage, ready to punish the one who wronged her son.

She looks at Clover's innocent face—the one who has endured so much—his nobility that has never questioned anyone's wrongdoing. Even now, he believes he deserves what he has received. She tilts her head down, positioning her face near his feet, a gesture of deep apology, expressing remorse not just for her own actions but for the wrongs committed by others as well.

"I'm so sorry, my baby," she says. "If I had just been brave, it would have protected you. If only I were…"

Clover stands up and backs away from Samantha. "Don't say sorry, Mom. I'm bad. A bad brother."

Brother.

Then it strikes her. Samantha was just telling Ethan about his big brother. Where has he gone? How did Clover end up in Ethan's place? Did Ethan leap out of the window, only for Clover to take his spot instantly?

Confused and concerned, she asks, "Where is Ethan? Did he jump out of the window?"

Clover is silent. What could he say in his defense? There isn't anything.

"Where is Ethan? Tell me, Nathan," she asks again, still politely.

Oddly, Samantha addresses Clover as Nathan, his rightful name, but he feels he does not deserve that name either. He isn't Nathan, and he isn't Verdi. Ethan is more deserving, yet Clover's greed has left him enmeshed in a Byzantine maze of problems.

Ethan is under the lake, and Clover doesn't know how. He hopes his fairy friend has arranged for him to breathe and holds a firm conviction that his younger sibling is faring well. Yet, in a secluded nook of his heart, there is a nagging awareness—a premonition that belies this belief—coaxing him that all is not as well as it seems.

He turns and sprints toward the door.

"Nathan, stop!" Samantha calls.

The door swings open, revealing Robert, his eyes deep and inscrutable, locked onto Clover. "You? What are you doing here in Ethan's bedroom?" he asks, his tone stern.

His confusion deepens as he shifts his scrutinizing gaze toward Samantha, who quickly averts her eyes.

"Sam?" he asks, entering the room. "What is this boy doing here?"

Samantha is afraid to look at him, wringing her hands, which angers Robert even more.

"I'm asking you something," he says, clenching his teeth.

Samantha gulps, her chest unable to contain her rapidly beating heart. She feels it might burst from her chest, yet secretly wishes it would, so she doesn't feel anything anymore. But she remains silent, her head lowered, until Robert forces it up.

"Tell me, where is my son?"

Samantha looks at Clover, who is nervously standing in the doorway, and something inside her triggers. She discovers an immense reservoir of strength she never knew she had.

She is no longer willing to endure the abuse and humiliation at the hands of her husband. In a moment of defiance, she twists his arm, causing his grip on her hair to slacken, and finally, she wrenches herself free from Robert's hold.

Her dark eyes blaze with high dudgeon, a glare devoid of love, fear, and submission. She unleashes a fierce roar directly into his face, a cathartic release of repressed emotions.

It stirs Robert. Samantha ultimately finds courage and pushes him to the ground with force. After enduring for so long, she finally summons the strength to fight back if necessary.

"Don't you dare touch me," she says, raising her finger at him once again.

Then she scans Clover; his mortified face says it all. "As for your son, he is right behind you."

Robert turns, perplexed not to find Ethan behind him. He only sees Clover and asks, "But that's Clover. Where is my son, Ethan?"

Samantha wears a nervous grin and squats down where Robert still lies recumbent, her hand reaching out for his hair and clutching it tightly, mimicking his cruelty.

He says nothing, just watches his wife retaliate.

"That's your son," she tells him. "Clover, a name that you gave him."

"A-a-h-h!" Robert gasps as she pulls his hair harder, forcing him to feel what it's like. "Leave me, Sam."

"Hurts, doesn't it?" Samantha smirks before releasing him.

Robert looks at her with horror, then massages his head, not worried about Samantha's rebellion but rather Clover's presence in their lives, as Ethan is nowhere to be found.

Samantha looks at Clover and beckons him to come forward. "Come, Nathan."

Clover steps forward reluctantly, wishing he could run away. But he knows he has to tell the truth.

Samantha places her hand on his head. "Tell me, Nathan, where is your little brother?"

Clover gulps and shivers, bowing his head. "Un—under the—the lake," he says, "with Lake Fairy."

Slowly, he lifts his head, meeting the appalled faces of Samantha and Robert, their mouths agape. Clover braces himself for punishment. "I—I took his place. Ethan is with Lake Fairy."

"Who is this Lake Fairy?" Robert barks, his jaw clenching. "And where is she? Why is Ethan with her?"

Clover shrinks away in fear.

"Don't scare him," Samantha says. "It is our fault." She pats Clover's head. "It's okay, my dear. Take us to him. We'll find him and bring him home. Okay?"

Clover nods but glances uneasily at Robert.

"I want my boy back." Robert shakes his head and storms outside, slamming the door shut.

"Come," Samantha grasps Clover's shoulders, "we'll bring your brother home."

Clover hesitantly walks out of Ethan's room. Samantha leads him downstairs and outside the mansion. Robert stands in the driveway talking to Mr. Manson.

Mr. Manson looks baffled to see Clover. "You?"

Robert has one hand on his hip and the other extended outward. "Keys, Arthur."

Mr. Manson hands the car keys to Robert while staring at Clover with his mouth open.

Robert gets into the driver's seat, rolls down the window, and bangs on the door. "What are you waiting for now?"

Samantha and Clover quickly settle into the backseat.

Robert speeds out of the driveway. "Where to, boy?" he asks Clover sternly.

Clover feels scared and cuddles closer to Samantha. "The—the lake. Kootenay Lake."

Samantha holds Clover tightly. "Don't talk to Nathan like that. He is just a boy."

"My boy is missing." Robert slams the brakes at a red light. "God forbid if anything happens to him, I'll show you both your place."

"He'll be fine," Samantha insists. "Nathan isn't a criminal or a plotter. Ethan is his little brother, and he knows that."

Clover's stomach churns, a nauseating sensation creeping up his throat. He feels overwhelmed by being referred to as the big brother when he clearly doesn't think he deserves it.

Meanwhile, Robert's hasty and erratic driving causes them to swerve back and forth, exacerbating Clover's discomfort. His heart races as Kootenay Lake gradually comes into view.

The path ahead proves too treacherous for the car to continue, forcing Robert to bring the vehicle to a stop.

Everyone steps out of the car.

"Now, where?" Robert asks.

Clover points to the lake. "Over there."

Robert runs his fingers through his hair in disbelief. "I'm telling you," he says with an edge to his voice, "if I don't find my son, I'll throw you both in that same lake."

Samantha pushes Clover behind her. "We'll find Ethan." She turns to Clover. "Lead us to your fairy friend, Nathan."

Clover takes the lead, forging a path through the dense vegetation and guiding his parents deeper into the escarpment. They walk amid the tall trees while the mist hovers thickly in the air, bringing a slight chill as they approach the lake.

The occasional sound of bears punctuates the silence, unsettling Robert. "Is he in these woods?" His voice trembles, and so does Clover's body.

Clover doesn't know exactly where Ethan is, but he confidently nears the shore of the lake and calls, "Lake Fairy!" His voice echoes back. He waits, but no response comes. "Lake Fairy, where are you?" It is yet another call—a plea, in fact.

No one responds again. Clover peers at the lake, scanning the waters for any sign of the fairy, hoping she will emerge with Ethan. However, the lake remains still, undisturbed, and no fairy appears. In a hopeful attempt to catch their attention, Clover picks up a small pebble and tosses it into the lake. The pebble breaks the surface, creating ripples that spread outward, but this action fails to awaken either the fairy or Ethan.

Clover shifts his gaze to the structure at the bottom of the lake, rumored to be the fairy's house. It stands unchanged, giving no hint of life or movement within. He begins to wonder if they are sleeping or if the fairy and Ethan are even there at all.

"Why are you throwing a rock?" Robert asks him calmly, though he is unnerved and shaking now. "Where is my son, Nathan?" He folds his hands. "Please, tell me."

"Find him, Nathan. Please do," Samantha begs, her voice quaking. "You're his older brother. Call your fairy friend."

"There is no fairy around," Robert barks. "We aren't living in a fairytale, are we? It's his imagination—just pure imagination. I bet he's done something to Ethan." He swallows hard. "Did you throw him into the lake to take his place?"

Clover shivers anxiously.

"But believe me," Robert groans, "you can never take his place."

"I—I didn't throw him in the lake," Clover says, shaking profusely. "I promise I didn't."

"Then find him," Robert shouts.

Clover stirs from his spot and runs toward the woods, going deeper where the Lake Fairy usually strolls, circling around each tree he finds and calling out for her, but there is no sign of her. Robert and Samantha join him in the forest, calling Ethan's name loudly. But the woods remain eerily silent. Samantha begins to wail, and Clover can hear Robert sobbing, too.

He feels terrible for causing this pain to Ethan's parents. He shouldn't have done what he did and wonders if the Lake Fairy isn't appearing because she thinks he still has the enchanted bag but is listening to him. "Lake Fairy," Clover calls loudly, "I don't have the bag with me. The spell is broken. Please come out with Ethan."

"The spell?" Samantha mutters, looking at Robert. "I don't understand."

Robert dashes to where Clover stands. "What spell?" he demands. "You just said the spell is broken. What's going on?"

Clover's eyes slide to Robert, noticing his pale face, furrowed brow, eyes filled with dread, and dry, parted lips. Clover deems himself a wretch, the architect of his brother's misfortune; he feels defeated, burdened by a weight as heavy as a mountain. He must bow to fate's whims. He cannot get the love he craves, the care and luxuries that led him to betray his friend, his little brother. The affection shown by Samantha was but a fleeting boon, destined to be the zenith of his fortune. The possibility of regaining his parents feels as distant as the stars, but he must do something to reverse their misery and bring back their worthy son.

In the thick of the woods, under the canopy of ancient trees, Clover runs wild, his feet crushing everything beneath them—dried leaves, broken branches, and small rocks. He leaps over the uneven ground, expertly avoiding the gnarled roots and hidden pitfalls in his path. His breath comes in short, sharp gasps, turning to vapor as he winds between the dense thicket of trees, racing toward the lake.

The sounds of his parents calling him to stop parrot in the air, yet he remains undeterred. Unstoppable in his momentum, Clover pushes on, regardless of the calls trailing behind him, until he reaches the lake. *If I go in, then Lake Fairy will have to come up. I should be the one living inside the lake, not Ethan,* he thinks.

And with a decisive plop, he dives into the lake, slicing through the blue waters.

Time stands still—the world pauses—as Robert and Samantha witness their elder child's impulsive plunge into the lake. They stand, momentarily frozen in disbelief and chaos. Then, they both start running toward the water's edge, with Robert's longer strides quickly outpacing Samantha. As he reaches the lake, the ripples from Clover's dive are just fading away.

Robert crouches at the water's edge, desperately searching for any sign of Clover beneath the surface. Finding nothing, he quickly sheds his blazer and plunges into the lake, his arms cutting through the water as he swims and dives, frantically trying to locate Clover.

Meanwhile, Samantha collapses to her knees on the shore, trembling in shock. Time stretches endlessly as Robert continues his frantic search in the deep water.

Finally, Robert resurfaces, gasping for air, his face ghostly and filled with exhaustion and fear. Keeping his hands on his knees, he turns toward Samantha. "It's too deep, the lake," he manages to say between heavy breaths. "I don't know where he is."

Samantha stifles a cry, shutting her eyes and shaking her head vigorously. "No, Nathan."

Robert joins Samantha at the shore, his clothes dripping wet. "He's gone," he says.

Their breaths are heavy, and their hope is fading. Not knowing what to do, they sit in silence. There is no sign of their children. Should they accept that they have become childless?

Robert looks for his blazer on the ground and thinks, *My cell phone.* He yanks out a large black phone from his pocket, ready to make a call, when a voice breaks through the silence.

"Mom! Dad!" Ethan appears, calling out to his parents.

"Ethan!" Robert drops his phone and rises to his feet.

Samantha stands up quickly, exclaiming, "Ethan! That's Ethan!"

Ethan runs toward them, throwing his arms around both of them in a tight hug with all the strength of his young being. Tears flow freely from all three. "I missed you both," Ethan says.

Robert lifts Ethan into his arms, holding him close. "I missed you too, my boy."

Slow footsteps begin to come closer. Samantha's ears perk up. She turns to see a tall figure approaching them—a woman with midnight-hued hair, straight as a horse's tail, mulberry lips, and pale skin.

"Alex, is that you?" Samantha takes nimble steps toward the woman.

Clover's Lake Fairy stands across from Ethan and Robert, dressed in black, her arms crossed, her crimson eyes staring right into them.

Robert places Ethan on the ground. "You?" he grunts, then looks at Samantha. "Was she here all along?"

Samantha shakes her head. "I don't know," she mutters.

"Yes, Robert," the fairy says. "Alex has been here since she was cast out by society. You'd think I have no means of surviving alone, wouldn't you? But here I am, with Mother Nature taking care of me."

Robert lunges forward. "What was Ethan doing with you?"

Alex cracks a twisted smile. "I have been taking care of him here in the woods." She winks at Ethan. "Tell them how much you liked living with me, my dear."

Ethan's eyes are filled with joy rather than fear. "Yes, Dad. She is great. She has a little house in the forest. We cook together and sing. She reads me stories, too."

Samantha closes in on her, pushing Ethan behind her. "How dare you, Alex? You stole my son."

Alex grins, snorting as her smirk turns into a sinister laugh. She clears her throat and says, "Let me tell you something, dear sister. I have also been taking care of your other son."

Samantha gasps, covering her mouth with her hand. "Are you his... Lake Fairy?"

Alex smirks, her chest heaving. "I'm Clover's Lake Fairy. The boy you left at the orphanage. Your son, your firstborn, Nathan."

Samantha stares at Alex in horror. "How—how?"

Alex lets out an evil laugh yet again. "Yes, he is my dear Clover."

Samantha screams, "No!"

Alex silences her laughter, looking at the bewildered faces of Samantha and Robert. "Where is he?" she asks. "He must have enjoyed a few days at your grand mansion. Ethan liked it but got bored and insisted on going home. Then we heard Clover's voice."

"Lake Fairy didn't want to leave her house, but I told her I wanted to go home," Ethan says. "Because we heard your voice, then Clover's."

"I didn't want to bring Ethan back to you." Alex steps forward, raising her finger. "Clover deserves to live in your mansion, just like Ethan. I know he's broken the enchantment. I was hesitant to come out, but do know, Samantha"—she pauses to catch her breath—"that your son has suffered, and it's time you both take him back with you. So, I'm here to make sure that happens today." She surveys her surroundings. "So? Where is my dear Clover?"

"Clover is gone," Samantha cries, collapsing to the ground and shrieking.

Alex hunkers beside her, her pale hands visibly shaking. "Gone? Where to?"

Ethan approaches and asks, "Where's Clover, Mom?"

Samantha pulls her cardigan together. "Alex, what did—what did you tell him?"

Alex's long, coffin-like nails dig into her cheeks. "What—what? I? What did I—"

"Stop lying, you cruel witch," Robert yells, then presses his lips together, resisting the urge to reveal the truth. "Clover jumped into the lake, looking for you or something. I jumped in too but couldn't find him anywhere. Poor thing, he is gone."

Alex's face turns even paler. "But why? Why did he jump into the lake?"

"Because you must have told him that you took Ethan under the lake, and he thought that's where you live," Samantha explains.

Alex shakes her head. "I never told him that. No, y—yes, I did tell him I take bad children into the lake, but... Oh no! No, Clover. What did you do? I told you I'd take care of your brother."

Flouncing her black gown, she plummets to the ground beside the shore, her hands raised, eyes misty with unshed tears. "What have you done?"

"You've proven you're nothing but a witch," Samantha stands up. "For years, I thought we wronged you. But no—you have surpassed the bounds of evil we had imagined."

"No—no," Alex whispers. "It can't happen."

Ethan crouches down beside Alex. "Why did Clover go into the lake?"

Alex is left with no answer.

Robert pats Ethan's shoulders and lifts him off the ground. "He is gone, Ethan. This woman, your auntie, is the reason for it."

"I don't understand," Ethan says, puzzled. "Will he never come up?"

Robert sighs. "Alex told Clover that she lived under the lake, lied to him, and he went there looking for you, my boy."

Alex remains anchored to the pebbled shore, her heart uttering cries.

"Do your magic, you witch," Samantha cries. "Bring my son back."

"I can't—I just can't," Alex sobs, regretting her friend's belief that she dwelled beneath the lake's surface. She peers into the lake and sings:

> "In winds so soft by the lake so still,
> Your Lake Fairy sits quietly with a hope so nil.
> Flutters my heart like invisible wings in plight,
> Awaiting you, my ally, through the day and night.
> Where have you gone, child, in these depths so deep?
> In the lake's cold cot, why do you sleep?"

Samantha emits a keening wail. Robert sheds a tear.

Alex gets up and runs along the shore. Through reeds and ripples, her gaze darts, each moment a dagger to her heart. She yearns for a sign in the eve's gloom, a feeble chance to see Clover rebloom. She drops to her knees and cries, "Come back to me from waters so stark. I'll guide you, guard you, never to part."

Her wish is granted as a clover leaf appears. Afloat on the lucid lake, the foliar charm comes near.

"I see something." Alex points to the clover leaf floating on the surface, her heart shattering into a million pieces as the leaf lands close to the shore.

It bears four leaves, an emerald crown, telling the tale of a boy drowned. With a heavy heart, beneath the sky's dim dome, the fairy weeps, knowing he won't come home.

Her magic is broken. An unblemished life her lies have taken. She holds the leaf, kisses it, giving silent adieu to an eternal spirit.

"I only told him that so he wouldn't force me to visit my house. I do magic, but my magic can't resurrect the departed. Forgive me, Samantha. Forgive me, Clover."